Born in Domblans in 1832, the socialist philosopher Fourier, who is credited with the first use of the word 'feminism', Marie-Louise Gagneur was a lifelong activist and a prolific and popular writer of fiction. Her education at a convent saw her develop strong anti-clerical views which she expressed in much of her writing. She wrote essays, short stories and more than 20 novels. She was made a Chevalier of the Légion d'Honneur in 1901 and died in 1902.

Anna Aitken studied French and German at St Peter's College, Oxford. Her previous translations include novels by Guillaume Musso and Caroline Vermalle.

Polly Mackintosh is an editorial assistant and translator. She has previously co-translated novels by Serge Joncour and Antoine Laurain.

Also available in the Revolutionary Women series:

Asphyxia by Violette Leduc
The Woman of the Wolf by Renée Vivien

THREE RIVAL SISTERS

THREE RIVAL SISTERS

By Marie-Louise Gagneur

Translated by Anna Aitken and Polly Mackintosh

Gallic Books
London

A Gallic Book

First published in France as *Trois Sœurs Rivales*, serialised in *La Presse* in
1861,

and *Une Expiation*, serialised in *Le Siècle* in 1859

First published in Great Britain in 2020 by Gallic Books
59 Ebury Street, London, SW1W 0NZ

A CIP record for this book is available from the British Library
ISBN 9781910477953

Typeset by Gallic Books

CONTENTS

THREE RIVAL SISTERS

I

The village of Domblans lay deep in a lovely verdant valley in the Jura. The houses were all tucked away discreetly behind layers of foliage, and from neighbouring hilltops one could just about make out brown roof tiles and the angular spire of the church through the dense line of poplars that wound its way along the river.

This valley lay in the foothills of the Jura, surrounded by lush green slopes. Further on, the sea of hills created a varied and picturesque scene filled with woodland, vineyards, terraced villages arranged in neat tiers, and scattered feudal ruins.

The undulating landscape, the warm, refreshing breeze and the tranquil surroundings softened the temperament of the labourer and calmed violent passions. This was a setting for languid daydreaming about imaginary lovers.

However, to the philosopher and the economist, this was no paradise. Did the excessive divisions and subdivisions of land that created a patchwork of irregular-shaped plots, the backward farming practices, the river that meandered across the landscape, covering it in swathes of gritty shingle, not all indicate a lack of organisation, competing interests and widespread poverty? Yet this was a place where the practice of intercropping would one day bring about bountiful production, intelligent and effective distribution, and yet more unimagined wonders in spite of man's efforts to destroy the land's innate charms.

The Château de Domblans, visited by Henri IV in 1595, was an elaborate monument to the days of feudal law. When all the fortresses were destroyed after Franche-Comté surrendered to Louis XIV, Domblans was allowed to remain, thanks to the ability of the châtelaine Gabrielle de Salines to charm the traitorous yet dashing Abbé de Watteville.

The residents of the valley barely noticed these vestiges of feudal times, but travellers passing through the region would stop to contemplate the remarkably uncracked stone of the ancient walls, the towers studded with arrow slits, the cross-shaped windows that recalled the Gothic style of the fifteenth century, ramparts that were still intact, and deep moats that had been converted into sloping orchards studded with fruit trees and carpeted with long grass.

A bridge over the moats connected the chateau and the garden. A steep grassy slope led down to the river that ran along the edge of the grounds. The Seille, whose waters had once run red with human blood, now flowed peacefully past, its whispers interrupted only by the gentle clicking sound of a watermill or the song of a nearby shepherd. Its waters ran clear, dulled only by the suds of local washerwomen.

Inside the chateau there were further delights to be found. The room in which Henri IV had once stayed was now called the 'Chambre Rouge', most likely after the scarlet painted patterns that covered the beams. The ceiling was white, and the letters 'C.R.' were repeated symmetrically across it, whilst on the yellow sides of the beams was the bitter sentiment 'Hope deceives'; the motto appeared twenty times, spaced out at neat intervals. An impressive fireplace bearing the combined coats of arms of the Charasssins and the Vautravers was painted with arabesques that matched the pattern on the beams. The doors were of sculpted oak and adorned with Gothic ornamentation. The country decor hinted at hours and days of careful work to create this scene.

Further points of interest in this remarkable room were a full-length portrait of Henri IV in cavalry dress, a handful of rusting trophies, a four-poster bed with fleur-de-lys patterned curtains, and a couple of moth-eaten armchairs.

The owner of the chateau, the Baron de Charassin, welcomed guests to this room with chivalrous courtesy. He never failed to reveal his admiration for the great king who had deigned to visit the ancestral seat of the Charassin-Vautravers, bowing his head respectfully before the inscription above the threshold of the Chambre Rouge which read '*In castello Domblanco Henricus magnus pernoctavit rex*'.

Monsieur de Charassin had served as a captain in the King's Guard under Charles X before retiring with his three daughters to Domblans, where he led the indolent life of a country nobleman with twenty thousand livres a year.

Much like his home, the retired soldier was a living anachronism, belonging to another age. He took little interest in the events of the day, preferring instead to live in hope of the return of the good old days.

For Monsieur de Charassin, Henri IV remained the model of a good monarch. The Baron loved to recall the story of the *poule au pot*, that kept alive the memory of the Béarn-born king in even the most humble country cottage, as he liked to say. This anecdote was perhaps more of a turn of phrase than historical fact.

There was, of course, something of the ridiculous in this unwavering admiration. Monsieur de Charassin endeavoured to imitate the king's airs and mannerisms and even claimed a physical resemblance with the monarch. His Bourbon nose and greying sculpted beard lent some validity to this claim; however, to the observer, his small, watery blue eyes were neither as piercing nor as discerning as those of the quick-witted Bourbon, his face had none of the intelligence, there was nothing about his expression that suggested power or intellectual vigour. He was narrow-minded and superficial, incapable of reflective or meaningful thought and his conversation consisted mainly of tired puns and bawdy anecdotes.

Our story begins in 1842 on one of those beautiful May mornings when the air is heavy with sweet scent and the sound of birdsong mingles with the bright colours of the spring. Monsieur de Charassin's three daughters were sitting under a flowered arbour, surrounded by honeysuckle and roses. Each with her own particular beauty, and radiating freshness and youth, this striking group amongst the flowers stood out against the gloomy and decaying spectre of the chateau behind them, whose decrepitude one might have expected to see reflected in its inhabitants.

The girls' conversation, normally light-hearted and easy, was today stilted and filled with long silences. They paid no attention to the embroidery in their laps, clearly distracted by some new topic. All three of them would look up at the slightest noise and every now and again one of them would gaze in the direction of the stony track that ran past the house and was separated from the garden by a low wall.

'Really, girls,' said one of them, most likely the eldest, in a mocking tone, 'the way the two of you have dressed yourselves, you'd think you were going to a ball. My dear Renée, your hair looks ridiculous with those plaits; you quite resemble the portrait of the medieval chatelaine in my father's room. As for you, my little Gabrielle, even if those short sleeves were apt for the season, I'm not sure I would be so eager to show Monsieur de Vaudrey those dark wrists that have been out in the sun all day.'

Gabrielle blushed as though her thoughts had been read, and looked at the ground. Then, deciding that there was no shame in the golden-brown hue of her delicate hand, took heart and responded sharply.

'Since you are so generously giving us advice, Henriette, grant us the pleasure of returning the favour. For it must be for Monsieur de Vaudrey's sake that you have decided to apply quite so much rouge to your cheeks. Renée and I remarked to each other just this morning that your pale complexion is so much more becoming to women of our class than the crude red that the village women paint on to their faces each day.'

Henriette bit her lip and glared at her sisters.

'You're lying!' she shrieked. 'I've never worn rouge in my life!'

'Ah,' said Renée, her tone gently malicious, 'so it's simply the prospect of seeing Monsieur de Vaudrey that's bringing colour to your cheeks?'

This sharp-tongued exchange was threatening to turn yet more venomous when they were interrupted by the sound of wheels on the path. Moved by the same curiosity, all three girls stood on tiptoe to peer over the wall between the garden and the lane. They sat down in simultaneous disappointment as a heavy ox-drawn cart trundled past the chateau.

Let us use the silence that followed this moment of dashed hopes to describe in more detail these three rather beautiful yet very different women.

Before that, however, a few words on the obvious animosity between Henriette and her two sisters.

Henriette was the daughter of Monsieur de Charassin's first wife. She had been raised by an aunt who taught her from a young age to regard Renée and Gabrielle with a mixture of disdain and jealousy.

Following her stepmother's death, Henriette returned to her paternal home at the age of twenty-one. She had a controlling and imperious nature and endeavoured to impress upon her sisters the superiority conferred on her by her age. Renée and Gabrielle therefore felt the need to unite against this common enemy, and so the three sisters were permanently at war, resulting in regular skirmishes and bitter exchanges.

Henriette was twenty-five years old, with brown hair. Her features, whilst less regular than those of her sisters, had nonetheless a certain refined and intelligent appeal. Unlike her sisters, she was not immediately beautiful, but beneath her rather forbidding exterior lay a passionate nature, and her energetic and sharp movements suggested a stormy temperament that had been rather suppressed by her upbringing. This upbringing had turned her natural tendency to moderate her behaviour into a cunningness that manifested itself in the thin line of her mouth and her dark, searching eyes. Her prominent chin and long face indicated a natural determination that tended towards stubbornness, and her thick dark eyebrows that would often draw together above her nose revealed her jealous spirit. Her luxuriant hair, golden skin and shapely figure gave her a Hispanic charm and hinted at an inner fieriness.

Renée, Monsieur de Charassin's second daughter, who was probably around twenty at the start of this story, provided a striking contrast to her sister. Her blonde hair gave her the look of one of Dürer's subjects and her face had a Germanic openness to it. Her blue eyes were pools of kindness and her high forehead and open features spoke of an innocent nature. Renée's every gesture exuded magnanimity and nobility; in other words, she was duty and devotion in human form. Henriette had once remarked that her calm, gentle manner and almost regal poise gave her the air of a medieval heroine, and that one could imagine her riding on a white steed, a falcon on her arm.

Gabrielle, for her part, seemed to be the link between Henriette and Renée, with elements of both temperaments in her nature. With Henriette she shared her fiery nature; with Renée her kindness. Her wide blue eyes seemed to sparkle with a childlike excitement. Her perfectly regular features were altered only by the flaring of her delicate nostrils. Her clear complexion, slender limbs, silken hair and long neck gave her an air of distinction and refinement.

This brief outline of the beauty of her two sisters leaves no doubt that Henriette, the eldest, and therefore most eager to find someone to appreciate her charms, was bitterly jealous of her two sisters, and that the flames of this jealousy were fanned yet further by the arrival of Monsieur de Vaudrey, a former ward of the Baron, and an eligible young man.

His arrival was a significant event for all three sisters, marking a break in the interminable solitude of their lives.

They had set about rejuvenating the interior of the castle, replacing the wall hangings in every wing, and pulling the silks from their dusty coverings. The newly polished oak furniture gleamed and spiders were shaken from their well-spun webs.

The garden received similar meticulous attention. As they carried out their tasks, the three sisters were spurred on by a common aim: to please Monsieur de Vaudrey and ensure that their antiquated home was to his liking. All three of them understood the import of a first impression, and so it was not without a measure of anxiety that they anticipated the arrival of the man who could bring to life the romantic fantasy each of them had been imagining from a young age.

As the eldest, Henriette believed she was more entitled to Monsieur de Vaudrey's heart than her sisters, and it never occurred to her that the heart is often deaf to such rights. However, she lived in fear of becoming an old maid, as she didn't know of any man within ten leagues that her father would accept as a son-in-law, rigorous as he was when it came to preserving the bloodline.

As Renée and Gabrielle prepared to welcome the visitor, their minds were not filled with thoughts of marriage; they were enjoying the thrill of the prospect of a little flirtation, a little intrigue, and perhaps even a taste of love.

They had been sitting in silence for about a quarter of an hour when Monsieur de Charassin appeared before them.

'Come now, Mesdemoiselles,' said the old man with an unintentionally comic flourish. 'I hope you are all ready to be most obliging to my guest. Monsieur de Vaudrey is a perfectly charming young man from a fine family. It may have been ten years since we last saw one another, but I take a particular interest in this gentleman and you will be pleasant to him for my sake. Now,' he said with a mischievous smile, 'which of you lovely things fancies herself as her ladyship the Madame de Vaudrey, wearing that noble crest, the crest that reads "*J'ai valu, je vaulx et vaudray*"?'

'But, Father,' said Renée, 'surely it is Monsieur de Vaudrey who will choose one of us, and we don't even know if …'

'Will Gabrielle be presenting herself too?' asked Henriette.

'I don't see why not,' replied Monsieur de Charassin, 'unless Gabrielle wishes to withdraw? In my day after all, the youngest often wouldn't marry at all, or was the last in the family to marry.'

These words revealed his secret wish to see Henriette, his favourite, married first.

'Oh Father, I'm too young to think of such things,' said Gabrielle in a nonchalant tone.

'Would you really have me believe, Gabrielle,' replied the Baron, 'that a girl of your age does not think about love at all? They say that young girls are more advanced than their male peers, and at your age I was certainly—'

'But, Father,' Henriette cut in, not wanting to miss the opportunity to remind her sisters of the rights of the eldest daughter so recently invoked by her father, 'is it not best for her to put such matters from her mind, since she will have to wait until the age of twenty-five as I did?'

'Don't worry, my dear girl,' said Monsieur de Charassin in a gallant tone, 'you are just as lovely as any girl of eighteen, and I am certain Monsieur de Vaudrey will share my feelings in this regard.'

The Baron then began a lengthy discourse on the de Vaudrey

bloodline, 'one of the first families of Franche-Comté, and one of the purest, free of any undesirable connection'. But we shall respectfully pass over this speech, being ourselves unversed in matters of heritage, bloodline, family crests or the marrying habits of the ruling classes, and lacking an understanding of the ways in which the science of heraldry can contribute to the improvement of the human condition.

When Monsieur de Charassin had left them, Gabrielle turned on her older sister, furious that she had, so to speak, been taken out of the running.

'I'd wager,' she said, 'that Monsieur de Vaudrey is as ugly as sin. What do you think, Renée?'

'I imagine him to be tall, slim and distinguished, with brown hair and dark eyes,' replied Renée.

'Not at all,' said Henriette sharply, 'he is sure to be blond and robust, with a powerful build like his forefather, the valiant Chevalier de Vaudrey, the terror of the tournaments. Knowing your foolish mind as I do, you probably think "distinguished" means pale and dreamy and consumptive and—'

'I fancy,' cried Gabrielle, 'that you're thinking of Joseph Duthiou, that handsome Hercules with his auburn hair, nothing "distinguished" about him, who sits behind us in church to receive your, shall we say, *benevolent* glances.'

A spark of hatred flared in her older sister's eyes.

'Why, you little snake!' she shrieked.

At that very moment they heard the crack of a whip as a carriage hurtled into the courtyard.

After a flurry of activity, the sisters once more took their places on the bench underneath the arch.

'May I warn you, my sweet,' said Henriette haughtily, 'that if

I hear such words from you again, I shall ensure that our father knows about it.'

'If there is no truth in my words,' replied Gabrielle, 'why do they anger you so? They were said purely in jest, yet your reaction might make one think that—'

'Well, know this, dear sister,' said Henriette sharply, 'I have little patience for such jokes and find them in the poorest taste; said in front of others your words could cause significant harm to my reputation.'

'Hush now,' whispered Renée. 'Stop quarrelling, here comes our father with Monsieur de Vaudrey.'

II

In the time it took for Monsieur de Vaudrey to make his way from the chateau to the arbour where the three girls sat they were able to establish that he was neither dark nor blond, nor tall nor powerfully built, but small and slender, with chestnut hair.

When he reached the bench where the three Charassin girls sat, they all appeared absorbed in their embroidery. Knowing nothing of the world, they were completely without guile and Monsieur de Vaudrey immediately felt the superiority that those with social graces and easy manners feel towards the meek and timid.

He was dressed impeccably in the latest style; aside from this detail there nothing remarkable about him. He was barely twenty-six, yet his tired expression, thinning hair and lined temples gave him the look of one five years older. His weak forehead indicated a feeble intellect, the round shape of his skull a prideful nature; his small hands and puny build were those of the runt of a noble breed. He was not especially ugly; his grey eyes, veiled and unreadable, hid his cold and calculating nature and his voice was rather attractive. He had been blessed with a good memory, and his conversation was peppered with platitudes and pleasantries that, on first meeting, passed for eloquence and refinement.

The sisters quickly abandoned their ideals of masculine beauty and after an hour or so of conversation found themselves all quite in thrall to Monsieur de Vaudrey, his apparent erudition and charming conversation compensating for his lack of physical allure.

As Henriette took his arm her attention was caught by a pair of eyes sparkling with resentment and jealousy staring at her through the foliage. She stumbled slightly, but quickly recovered herself, making an almost imperceptible gesture to the hidden figure, and continued on to the chateau.

Once he was alone, the man who had caught Henriette's eye stood up and crept through the trees until he reached the far end of the wall, assured himself that he was out of sight and leapt over it. Dejected and disappointed, he trudged home with the air of a man suddenly faced with the difficulty of acquiring what he has always wanted.

'Joseph!' called out a local man with a crafty look about him. 'Have you heard the news?'

Joseph Duthiou, for this was indeed the man who had been the subject of Gabrielle's little quarrel with Henriette, paused and, although he feared he already knew what this news would be, responded: 'No, I haven't. What is the news?'

'We saw a very fine carriage passing through, and they say it belongs to a man who has come to ask for Henriette's hand.'

'I see,' replied Joseph, blushing. 'And what business is that of mine?'

'None I dare say; nor is it any of mine,' said the peasant with a mocking smile and the wink of a man who knows he is speaking out of turn.

Joseph continued his slow walk back to the village.

He was a handsome man and undeserving of Gabrielle's mockery. He wore the garments of a man of his class, but he carried himself with a casual nonchalance that had none of the stoop of the honest labourer who spends his days working the land. His demeanour hinted at a gentler and more refined spirit than that of the working class, of which he appeared to be a member. He had regular features and an intelligent expression, dark eyes, golden skin and thick hair of that shade of auburn so beloved of painters. At first glance these features suggested a passionate and sentimental nature, but the more discerning observer perceived in his expressions and the small movements of his lips not romance and fire, but cunning and ambition. In fact, despite his strong features and sturdy frame, there was something idle and effeminate about the man. These contrasting forces in his nature were evident in what Joseph Duthiou had eventually chosen for his profession. Intelligent and determined to improve his lot, Joseph had left his father's farm at a young age to learn a trade in town.

Having found employment painting walls and exteriors, his eye for design meant that he was soon elevated to the rank of interior decorator.

After he had completed his tour of the country, he returned to his family home with the intention of paying only a brief visit. It is this moment in time, around six months before Paul de Vaudrey arrived in Domblans, that marks the beginning of our little intrigue.

It is necessary to shed some light on these preceding events as they inevitably came to cast a long shadow over Henriette's fate.

Whether out of diplomacy or genuine goodwill, Monsieur de Charassin had always displayed courtesy and warmth to the villagers, and he adhered to ancient custom by sending his daughters to open the village dances. Deprived as they were of any other social entertainment, the Charassin girls threw themselves into these occasions, setting aside any feeling of superiority and joining in the dances with unselfconscious joy.

It was at one of these village gatherings that Henriette saw Joseph for the first time. His handsome looks and air of refinement caught her attention immediately. Joseph was quick to notice her glances and soon felt emboldened to meet her gaze.

Joseph's stay was prolonged by the decorative works he had been asked to carry out in the village church. A few skilfully painted cherubs were enough to win Henriette's admiration, and she believed she had discovered a unique artistic talent.

Prior to this, Henriette's imagination, deprived of any other stimulation in the leisurely torpor of her life in the chateau, had roamed far and wide, tormented by emotions she could not name. She had read a handful of novels, among them *Le Compagnon du Tour de France*. The dazzling image of Pierre Hugenin, the skilled tradesman, was the inspiration for her reveries and she spent her days inventing a pastoral romance in which she was the swooning heroine and Joseph Duthiou the dashing hero.

In order to perpetuate her republican fantasy, Henriette persuaded her father to have Joseph restore some of the paintings in the Chambre Rouge. The love story was all but complete.

What began as a feigned interest in the restoration process and conversations regarding what was still to be done quickly became passionate and intimate discussions about inequality and poor working conditions, during the course of which, it must be noted,

Joseph demonstrated none of Pierre Hugenin's characteristic sharpness or honesty. These exchanges then became letters passed back and forth in utmost secrecy and furtive rendezvous under cover of darkness in the garden.

Around this time Henriette furthermore dedicated herself publicly to improving the plight of the villagers, greeting each one with warm familiarity, and she was often to be heard decrying the prejudices of the nobility and extolling the many virtues of the working class. Monsieur de Charassin bridled at his daughter's revolutionary speeches and egalitarian posturing, which secretly delighted Henriette, although she assumed the guise of a tragically misunderstood martyr.

Although on first impression a liaison of the kind we describe may seem unlikely, it is not difficult to discover a reasonable explanation for it. Throughout the countryside one finds instances of female members of the aristocracy condescending in such a way to commoners.

A curious psychological phenomenon! And surely one of the more imperious urges of the heart, as Voltaire reminds us: 'The need to love is such that one projects one's soul on to the most unworthy of objects!'

Could this perhaps be an effect of the inferior education provided to provincial girls of the noble class, the product of a mind too little occupied and insufficiently stimulated? Or perhaps this is the impact of our foremost institutions, so imbued with egalitarian principles, on the mores of our ancient nobility, which have up until this point proved so impervious to social change? It is perhaps a combination of all of these influences.

When Monsieur de Charassin first announced to his daughters the impending arrival of his ward, Henriette's passion for social justice had, if not dissipated, cooled somewhat. She started to think seriously about the potential consequences of her affair with Joseph Duthiou. She had started to find some of her lover's manners rather coarse, and was beginning to sense that a truly mutual relationship was impossible without a certain parity of education and sensibility, if not of social standing. She therefore looked on the prospect of marrying Monsieur de Vaudrey as a means of safeguarding her position in society and her dignity. But she had quite forgotten the rash promises she had made to Joseph, and the ambition that her attentions had awakened in him.

III

Let us return to Paul de Vaudrey, beginning with a short account of his life thus far.

Orphaned as a child, he was sent to Paris for his education where before too long he managed to squander most of his inheritance. By the time he turned twenty-six he felt that he had experienced all that Paris had to offer him and that his modest means no longer afforded him the dignity demanded by the family name. He therefore decided to return to his ancestral seat and play lord of the manor. Before he could do this, however, he planned to visit Domblans with the intention of repairing the damage done to his fortune by his youthful excesses with an advantageous marriage to one of the Charassin girls.

When he had written to his guardian to enquire as to his feelings about the intended visit, the Baron had replied with three words: 'Come, see, conquer.'

In the manner of most mediocre men he was confident that he would not leave unsuccessful. Bolstered by a handful of conquests in Paris, he felt certain he would easily charm naive country bumpkins who were doubtless languishing in boredom and solitude. To ensure his success, he thought it best to court all three sisters at once. He would shower each one with affection, giving her the consideration and attention that all women so craved, and these efforts would surely suffice to turn the heads of these poor girls, starved as they were of any other pleasure.

However, when he found himself in the midst of three such delectable, and pleasingly modest, young women he had to admit to himself that he was not as impervious to emotion as he had fancied. Their unexpected beauty was a welcome addition to the promise of the dowry, and he made a solemn oath to himself that at least one of the girls would fall deeply in love with him before the eight days were up.

His vanity was inflated yet further when after a few days he realised the extent to which all three girls endeavoured to please him. He was now utterly convinced of his own success. From that moment on he basked in his victory and took pleasure in toying with his victims, giving no thought to the destructive power of passion on a young heart unused to the world and overflowing with love.

Countless examples have shown how rarely the life of seclusion and solitude that is the lot of so many young women in France leads to a life of tranquillity and happiness, contrary to the assumptions of over-protective parents. Young girls, their heads filled with stories of great loves, are deprived of their freedom, raised in baneful ignorance of the world around them, and carefully shut away to protect them from dangers that their inexperience leaves them unable to confront. Yet sooner or later, things follow their natural course and these heavenly creatures with their loving hearts inevitably give themselves passionately to the first man they encounter. Thus ensue years of cruel disillusionment, painful disappointment and bitter regrets that are enough to leave a young life quite ruined.

Are not the English and American customs that grant young women so many freedoms more practical by far? These women may have less virtue, but with a better understanding of what they are undertaking do they not also have far greater chances of future happiness?

A fortnight after his arrival at Domblans, Paul de Vaudrey found himself once again with the Charassin girls in the very same arbour under which he had first made their acquaintance.

He was telling them about love.

Monsieur de Vaudrey sat between Renée and Gabrielle, seeming to pay particular attention to the youngest of the group. This was perhaps intended to provoke Renée, whose proud nature meant that her demeanour remained cold even as her affection for him grew, or perhaps to arouse the jealousy of the eldest sister Henriette, whose coquettish airs amused him.

After a lengthy and relatively commonplace discourse on the matter, he turned to Gabrielle and fixed her with a passionate stare.

'And you, Gabrielle, what have you to say about love?'

Gabrielle raised her eyes to meet Monsieur de Vaudrey's gaze. Startled by its intensity, she dropped her embroidery; as they both bent down to pick up the fallen cloth, their heads touched and Gabrielle's happiness was complete.

'My dear Gabrielle,' he insisted gently, 'will you not answer my question?'

The poor child felt as though she might faint.

'M-me,' she stuttered, 'I suppose, I, well, I suppose I have never given it much thought. Love scares me, I think, and I don't know why. I am afraid of finding it.'

'My dear girl,' said Henriette, who had noticed the silent exchange between Paul and Gabrielle, 'the fear in your voice would lead one to believe that you have reason to be afraid. Could it be that someone has already disappointed you?'

'Perhaps it is a premonition,' murmured Gabrielle, suddenly overcome with despair.

'And you, Henriette,' said Monsieur de Vaudrey, turning his back on Gabrielle, 'what is your conception of love?'

'Perhaps I have misspoken and offended him!' Gabrielle thought to herself, having dared for a moment to believe she was the favourite.

'To formulate an opinion on an emotion, one must first have experienced it,' replied Henriette in a righteous tone. 'I myself have never been in love, and shall only love the man I marry. I was brought up to believe that it is a woman's duty to love her husband, raise children and devote herself to her family. Therefore, I believe that love is equal to devotion.'

'Mademoiselle, the man who has the honour of marrying you is a lucky fellow indeed,' said Paul with a gallant bow that hid his disdain for this bourgeois declaration.

'Oh, you are too kind!' exclaimed Henriette, and, with an air of false modesty, 'Of course, I do have my flaws.'

'To a man in love, a woman's flaws are part of her perfection,' replied Paul.

When Gabrielle noticed Paul and Henriette exchanging glances, as she and he had done but moments earlier, she could not stop a tear running down her cheek.

'And now to you, Renée,' continued Monsieur de Vaudrey,

'may I, at the risk of being either dull or indiscreet, permit myself to ask you the same question as your sisters?'

'For my part,' replied the innocent girl calmly, 'I believe that love is the most beautiful and most pure of human sentiments, and although I know my sister Henriette shall surely mock me for my whimsical nature, for she loves to accuse me of fancying myself a medieval heroine, I dream of a great romance, one of those love stories we learn about from the Crusades, a love that can withstand absence and that leaves one a braver and more noble individual.'

'Oh, Renée,' cried Paul with perfectly calculated enthusiasm, 'if these were the days of the Crusades I would be honoured to wear your colours!'

'Who is his favourite?' was the question playing on the minds of the three girls, a question none of them were able to answer.

This moment marked the beginning of a rivalry between the three sisters, a rivalry with most unhappy consequences.

In accordance with the fact, perhaps even the tradition, of parents not understanding their own children, Monsieur de Charassin, far from being concerned at this rivalry, actively encouraged it. He sang his ward's praises at every opportunity and declared himself impressed by the man's charming and verbose style of conversation, and made clear his desire to have a son-in-law capable of such elevated discourse. This was, of course, all in addition to his noble blood and understanding of heraldry.

With this paternal encouragement, love blossomed in the hearts of the three girls. Each of them experienced this emotion in their own particular way. For Henriette, love was a calculation that was all-consuming in its egotism. This was further complicated by her relentless desire to end the spinsterhood that had been imposed on her. She was simultaneously gripped with fear over her young lover in the village, who since the arrival of Paul de Vaudrey in Domblans had taken to writing her jealous letters filled with threats.

Renée's love was as pure and refined as her own nature. It was a tranquil and generous feeling, characterised by devotion rather than jealous passion.

But Gabrielle, with her sensitive disposition, vivid imagination and a loving nature that bordered on the obsessive, longed to find love as a prisoner longs for freedom and fresh air. She was like a carnation whose stem drooped under the weight of too many petals; she felt burdened by her overflowing heart. Her steps became slow and heavy and her shoulders stooped, her eyes were glassy and her gaze feverish, her pink nostrils flared occasionally as if she were drinking in some hidden pleasure from the air, she laughed or cried hysterically at the slightest provocation. And then Paul de Vaudrey would take her hand and look into her eyes with an expression that made her tremble. She was in love with him, and adored him with all the impulse and virginal devotion of first love.

Yet a month had passed, and Monsieur de Vaudrey had still not made his choice.

Henriette intrigued him with her complex and secretive nature, although his intuition suggested she was fundamentally selfish.

All living beings absorb and radiate vitality in their own way. This process is an unconscious act of the will and takes place throughout the body, and explains why one often senses a cold aura when in the presence of a selfish person, who absorbs more than they radiate, whereas in the presence of a kind soul we tend to feel a gentle warmth that invites our sympathies.

Paul therefore hesitated only in choosing between Renée and Gabrielle. Renée, regal and reserved, seemed to demand his respect and presented a challenge to his pride. Gabrielle, on the other hand, awakened in him a more sensual admiration.

Henriette had not failed to notice that her sisters outranked her in Monsieur de Vaudrey's affections, yet she still nursed a hope that she would be his bride, and resolved to compensate for what she lacked in physical charms with cunning and artfulness. Gabrielle was her principal rival, as she felt sure she could easily outshine the reserved Renée. Whenever she saw one of them in the company of Monsieur de Vaudrey, her heart swelled with a spiteful, vengeful envy.

One balmy evening in June, Monsieur de Vaudrey rode into the grounds on horseback, returning from a ride in the countryside. He selected a garden bench and sat deep in thought, ruminating his matrimonial plans. It was clear that he could not prolong his stay at Domblans any further without making some kind of offer to Monsieur de Charassin, who became daily more impatient to know the outcome of his decision. For the twentieth time, he reflected on the choice between Gabrielle and Renée. He found the two girls equally beautiful, equally sympathetic in nature, and for what felt like the hundredth time he found himself unable to decide between the two. At that moment, however, he caught sight of Gabrielle turning down one of the garden paths. Determined to understand this sudden apparition as a heavenly intervention, he decided to take advantage of the moment to declare his intentions to Gabrielle.

She looked particularly beautiful that evening. Since Monsieur de Vaudrey's arrival, she had gradually and unwittingly taken on the appearance of one in love, changing and evolving with each new day; her face, already fresh and flushed with youth, had taken on a languorous quality that brought a certain poetry to her features.

As she drew closer to Paul, her slow, melancholy gait gave her the look of someone bearing the great burden of unrequited love.

She had in fact come to this part of the garden in the hope of finding Monsieur de Vaudrey there, as he had been nowhere to be seen that afternoon. When she caught sight of him, however, she did what any woman in such circumstances would, and pretended to be deep in thought, concealing her excitement at finding him there.

'Monsieur Paul,' she said, 'do you happen to know where I could find my sisters?'

'No, I have seen neither of them this afternoon,' responded Monsieur de Vaudrey. 'But please, sit for a moment, Gabrielle, I should like very much to speak with you.' Taking her hand, he pulled her gently down on to the bench next to him.

'What could you have to say to me that could cause you to look so solemn?' said Gabrielle, noticing his grave expression.

It had been some time since Monsieur de Vaudrey had felt quite so overcome with emotion; he was now perfectly convinced of his love for her. For a moment, he simply looked at Gabrielle. In that instant, she was all grace and poetry. Her lustrous brown hair shimmered in the dewy evening air, falling perfectly on her breast as she looked tremblingly into Paul's adoring eyes. The fading sunlight illuminated her translucent complexion and sparkled in the pearly blue of her eyes, which shone with a combination of desire and modesty. Soft dimples appeared in her cheeks as she smiled at him.

As he gazed at her, he could not stop himself exclaiming: 'Oh Gabrielle, how beautiful you are!'

This exclamation left the poor child somewhat dazed, and she tried to disguise her distress by replying with a nervous laugh that revealed her shock.

'If that is all you have to say to me, I shall leave you in peace,' she said, standing up as if to leave.

'Please, Gabrielle, I beg of you!' said Paul, holding her hand to keep her with him. 'Stay a little longer, and let me open my heart to you.'

Gabrielle took up her seat again but, sensing danger, said: 'Speak quickly, for I must go and find my sisters.'

Paul took both of the young girl's hands in one of his and pulled her close to him with the other.

'Well then, I will have to hold you captive, my little savage, for I have something very serious to tell you that is of as much import to you as it is to me,' he said, pressing his lips to her hair.

At that moment they were startled by the sound of leaves rustling behind them.

'Someone is there!' cried Gabrielle, her face flushing scarlet.

'What of it, my dear?' replied Paul. 'Tomorrow, all the world will know of our love for one another. For you do love me, don't you, Gabrielle?'

'Oh, I do,' she replied with childlike ease.

She had barely finished speaking when Henriette appeared before them. She had heard everything.

'Aha! There you both are,' she said in a perfectly practised tone of surprise. 'It will soon be supper time; are you not a little cold sitting outside like this?' then, addressing Monsieur de Vaudrey: 'What became of you this afternoon?'

'I rode to pay a visit to the caves at Baume, after you recommended them to me. Those huge carved stones towering over the dell are a strange sight indeed. There was a great deal of water gushing from the mouth of the cave, so I was unable to climb the fragile ladder that leads up to the entrance and see the lake concealed inside it. I was quite fatigued upon my return and so chose to sit here awhile until supper.'

'Gabrielle, you are quite pale!' exclaimed Henriette in a concerned tone. 'Are you unwell?'

'Me? Oh, no, not at all!' said Gabrielle, as though she were emerging from a dream-filled sleep.

To prevent Henriette from asking any more uncomfortable questions, Paul quickly resumed his description of his ride that day.

At the dinner table, he was lively and jovial, holding forth to the assembled company, while Gabrielle remained consumed by her happiness. She did not dare speak or meet anyone's gaze for fear that her tone or expression would reveal the joy in her heart. She was astonished that Paul was able to appear so light-hearted. 'If he were as overjoyed and moved as I, he would not be able to speak as he does now.' Her spirits sank as she realised that Paul's love for her could not possibly be as powerful as hers for him.

In truth, Monsieur de Vaudrey was incapable of truly loving anyone; in his case, love was nothing more than a manifestation of his selfishness. Since their exchange in the grounds he had already begun to have doubts about Gabrielle. Had she not perhaps too eagerly accepted his declaration of love? She suddenly appeared terribly young and naive. He was now beginning to regret his haste in making a decision and considered himself lucky that Henriette had interrupted them at that precise moment, saving him from a path from which there might have been no return as far as Gabrielle was concerned. Suddenly, Renée seemed a much more appealing prospect than her younger sister; her calm and dignified demeanour was surely preferable to her younger sister's excessive impressionability.

That evening, Renée had coquettishly placed some flowers from the garden in her golden hair, perfectly setting off her delicate complexion. Her smile revealed a kind and gentle nature and her candid gaze aroused a desire in the otherwise impervious man to disturb her virginal serenity. Her apparent coldness to Monsieur de Vaudrey inflamed his vanity; he was determined to overcome her pride and subject this creature, whom he knew to be his superior, to his inferior will. He therefore altered his intentions and made Renée the sole object of his attentions and tender looks.

Gabrielle, unaware as she was of this plotting, initially believed that her beloved, for reasons she could not divine, was acting in such a way in order to conceal his true feelings from the assembled company. Soon, however, jealousy crept into her heart and she paid dearly for her fleeting taste of happiness in the garden. Unable to withstand the weight of her own suffering, she left the dining room to hide her tears.

Henriette was not sure what to think, but she delighted in her sister's distress and took comfort in the thought that even if Paul was indifferent to her, she would easily break the false or at least superficial attachment he had towards her two rivals.

IV

That night all three sisters were unable to sleep, each one reflecting on the events of the evening in her bedroom. A vague sense of premonition kept them from slumber, the sense that they were about to experience a moment that would alter irrevocably the course of their existence.

Gabrielle wiped away her tears and took heart, for the night is propitious to both sorrow and hope.

'Perhaps,' she thought to herself, 'he means to test my love for him. He must love me; he would not be so cruel as to— No, he cannot be deceiving me; he was as moved as I was; his voice trembled as he spoke. And did he not promise me that tomorrow everyone would know of our love?'

But her jealousy soon returned and her cheeks were wet with tears again. She spent the rest of the night consumed by painful apprehensions and delicious memories.

When Renée had returned to her bedroom she undressed, put on a white robe and sat gazing out of her window.

The air was warm and scented, and the moon shone brightly against the dark blue of the sky, illuminating shapes and shadows that only encouraged the girl's fantastical imagination. Her mind was also preoccupied with romance and the evening had given her reason to hope; she opened her heart to the night-time air and revealed her secrets to it. The outline of her slender frame in the arched Gothic window gave her the look of a medieval heroine waiting to be saved, or of a faithful wife praying for her husband's swift return.

Renée was drawn out of her reverie by what looked to be a shadow stealing between the bushes in the garden. Despite her dismay, she tried to make out who the strange apparition could be. The mysterious figure soon moved into the moonlight and she recognised Henriette's silhouette. She was greatly surprised and, intrigued to discover why Henriette should be in the garden at such an advanced hour, she gently pushed open her window and fixed her gaze on the scene unfolding below her. She was further astonished to see her sister pull a stone from the wall and remove a piece of paper that had been hidden beneath it, tucking it furtively into her dress.

Renée sat for some time trying to guess what this mysterious piece of paper could be. Her first instinct was jealousy. Perhaps this was a letter from Monsieur de Vaudrey; perhaps his attentiveness that evening had been nothing more than a pretence to conceal his true affections. This new thought made sleep impossible for the young girl and she spent the remainder of the night torturing herself with the most far-fetched conjectures.

Let us, then, attempt to divine the nature of Henriette's secret. She had left the dining room at the end of the evening in a bitter mood. 'Who is it that he loves? Gabrielle? Renée?' she thought to herself. 'No, it is more likely that he loves none of us; he is far too conceited. He must truly despise me, as he does not even pretend to show me affection as he does with my sisters, and yet I would accept even false attention from him. He seems to hate me and I do not know why. But what is to be done?' she thought to herself, taking heart. 'I love him, and I shall be his bride. Then I shall truly love him. Better still, I shall have my revenge and make him regret the day he slighted me. But first I must marry him. How is it to be done?'

She was sitting on a low chair, still in her evening dress. She leaned forward and put her head in her hands, deep in thought. She stood up suddenly as though she had just remembered something of great import, put on a coat and crept down the stairs that led to the garden. When she returned from the excursion to which Renée had, unbeknownst to her, been a witness, she quietly slipped back into her bedroom to read the missive that had so intrigued her younger sister.

The letter was from her village paramour who now inspired in her nothing but repugnance mixed with shame. However, during the six months that had marked the duration of their affair, they had used a small opening in the garden wall as a means of exchanging their *billets-doux*.

In this particular note the ambitious craftsman, sensing a rival in Monsieur de Vaudrey, accused Henriette of coldness and disdain towards himself and ended the letter by demanding she meet him in a secluded part of the grounds between ten and eleven o'clock the following Thursday, threatening revenge should she refuse his request.

Henriette crumpled the piece of paper in her hands and, instead of putting it on the fire, cast it aside indignantly.

She knew him well enough to know that his threats were not

to be taken lightly and resolved to meet him at the appointed hour, in order to avoid a scandal. 'How foolish I have been!' she thought to herself. 'How low this connection might have dragged me, had it been allowed to continue! How debasing to be the object of reproach of a peasant! I, a Charassin! How could I have forgotten myself so? If my father were to find out …'

And then, she had a thought.

'Perhaps I shall be able to use this shameful episode to my benefit.'

She sat deep in thought for a while. By the time the church bells sounded at three o'clock she had formulated her plan; she promptly went to bed and slept soundly until half past six the following morning.

V

She arose quickly and dressed, then went directly to her father's rooms. She hesitated for a moment before entering but soon strengthened her resolve and pushed open the door.

Monsieur de Charassin sat enveloped in a large night-robe on an antique armchair, contentedly watching long plumes of smoke billow from a clay pipe.

When Henriette entered, he laid down his pipe and bowed to his daughter with the antiquated formality that was his custom even with his daughters.

'Awake so early!' he greeted her. 'What news could possibly bring you to my door at such an hour?'

Henriette kissed her father and answered in a trembling voice.

'It is something truly terrible, Father. I am not even sure I will be able to tell you, for fear of your temper.'

'Come now, child,' replied the good Baron with paternal warmth, 'when have I given you cause to fear me? Tell me at once; you have my undivided attention.'

When Henriette still seemed reluctant, Monsieur de Charassin pulled her on to his lap and kissed her forehead.

The girl was particularly dear to him as she reminded him of her mother, his first wife, with whom he had been very much in love.

Like all weak men, the old Baron was excessively protective of his authority. The slightest attempt to challenge it openly left him furious. However, he was easily swayed by anyone with enough wit to use more subtle means to undermine him. Henriette, who had been blessed with the gifts of perception and cunning, perfectly understood his nature and was thus able to manipulate her dull-witted father without difficulty.

Today she was on fine form, playing the role of the young innocent to perfection. Tears rolled down her face as she nestled her head on the Baron's shoulder, allowing her beautiful hair, which she knew he loved, to fan out around them.

'Why, it is as though she were here with us again!' he cried. 'Your hair and figure are the very picture of your dear mother.'

'In the name of my mother, whom you loved so deeply, I beg you to forgive the pain that I am about to cause you,' pleaded Henriette, taking her father's hands in hers and staring up at him imploringly. Monsieur Charassin was utterly taken in by the disingenuous display.

'Tell me at once, my child! If it is needed, rest assured my forgiveness is yours but please spare me this torturous preamble!'

'At least,' sobbed Henriette theatrically, throwing her arms around his neck, 'I am able to embrace you one last time before you surely renounce me!'

'Heaven and earth! Do you mean to bring me to tears, child?'

'Father,' replied Henriette, standing up with dignity, 'I shall reveal all to you no matter the cost, and should it be required I shall endeavour to resist your anger, for this is a matter of not only my happiness, but the happiness of another.'

These words seemed an open affront to the Baron's authority and Monsieur de Charassin was on the point of rage when he suddenly reflected and said in a calm and cheerful tone: 'Aha! I believe I understand you perfectly. I am only surprised that I suspected nothing before this moment! Might I venture that you are speaking of marriage?'

'But, Father, how could you have guessed?' replied Henriette with just the right amount of shame in her voice.

'How could I fail to guess this was the purpose of your visit!' cried the Baron. 'Do you take me for an imbecile or think me blind? My child, I have guessed everything. There is nothing you can teach an old soldier such as myself about matters of the heart. This union was my dearest wish and I consent to it with all my soul, for Monsieur de Vaudrey was indeed the man I had—'

'But Father!' Henriette cut in, hiding her face in her hands. 'Please, I do not deserve your goodwill. I cannot bear to hide the truth from you any longer.'

'I see,' replied Monsieur de Charassin, his face darkening. 'What other match can you speak of? I know of no other suitors than Monsieur de Vaudrey.'

'Ah but, Father, you do know this man,' she said. 'For I am speaking of Joseph Duthiou.'

'Joseph Duthiou!' exclaimed the old nobleman, his eyes widening in shock.

However, he soon recovered himself and continued.

'You must explain yourself properly, child, instead of subjecting me to such unkind misapprehensions. You doubtless meant to say that you intend to have Jeannette, your maid, marry Joseph Duthiou and you have come to seek my permission, and perhaps even a small dowry for the girl. Well, I gladly give my consent, and shall leave you to arrange the matter as you see fit.'

'No, Father, you have misunderstood me!' replied Henriette passionately. 'It is I who wish to marry Joseph Duthiou.'

'Ah, an excellent jest!' replied the Baron, with a rich chuckle. 'A clever trick. Tell me the joke in full, my love, and I promise I shall laugh heartily.'

'Your miscomprehension and your light-heartedness cause me to suffer greatly,' said Henriette. 'I do not jest, my will is set, and if you require further proof of my affections, here it is.'

With these words, she placed a selection of Joseph Duthiou's letters to her in his lap.

'As you will see, Father,' she continued, 'our association has up until now obeyed the laws of propriety.'

Monsieur de Charassin rapidly cast his eye over the contents of the letters, then crumpled them in his hands in fury.

'The Lord have mercy!' he cried. 'A liaison between a Charassin and a peasant? You have taken leave of your senses.'

Still pronouncing threats and curses, he took his pipe and hurled it to the floor, a sure sign of extreme indignation.

The canny young girl sat very still, her composure indicating a steel-like determination and strength of will.

'Father,' she began in a self-righteous tone, 'I am afraid to say you are quite out of touch with the age we live in. We are no longer in the fifteenth century; there are no peasants and noblemen any more. We do not distinguish between the classes, and the privileges once enjoyed by the nobility exist only in your imagination.'

Upon hearing this reasoning, the Baron became apoplectic with rage.

'Do you hear these words, ancestors?' he cried out. 'Do you

hear the way my daughter speaks? The nobility, a figment of my imagination! As far as you are concerned three generations of noble blood and a title inherited from Charles of Burgundy are mere chimeras! A curse! A curse upon my name! I made a grave error when I married your mother; she was born of a lowly people. I married her during the Spanish War. I was blinded by passion and forgot my rank and raised up from nothing a woman of no standing at all. But bad blood will out; you are only too like her, unworthy of the Charassin and Vautravers names. I curse the day you were born! You are no daughter of mine.'

Overwhelmed by the vehemence of this emphatic discourse, the poor Baron collapsed into his armchair in a state of profound exhaustion. Such fits of pique are characteristic of weak men and are most often followed by some form of reaction. Henriette knew that she had sufficiently upset her father and consequently prostrated herself at his feet.

'Father, my dear Father,' she sobbed, 'I must beg your forgiveness, for I am less culpable than it may appear. Please do not think me ungrateful. Revealing my secret to you has caused me no small amount of suffering.'

The Baron was implacable.

'I beg you, a word to show your forgiveness,' she implored him.

The Baron was satisfied with this response. He lowered his gaze and turned away from her.

'My goodness, how like your mother you are. Come, child, embrace me. You will forget this folly, do you understand me?'

'Father, if I might say a word in my defence?' said Henriette timidly.

'Enough, we shall hear no more of this ridiculous intrigue,' the Baron interjected firmly. 'My will is that you shall marry Monsieur de Vaudrey. This alone will allow me to forgive the great pain you have just caused me to suffer. I shall speak with Paul today.'

Henriette was taken aback by such a prompt and exact realisation of her wishes. She attempted to conceal her joy behind an attitude of dutiful resignation.

'Father, I will do as you ask of me, of course, but—'

'My dearest!' cried the happy father, pulling her into his arms. 'I assure you I have forgotten everything.'

'Of course, Father. But allow me to bring one obstacle to your attention. Monsieur de Vaudrey does not love me.'

'He does not love you? I cannot believe this to be true, my lovely girl. An unlikely state of affairs, certainly. Still, if this is the only obstacle, consider it removed; I give you my word,' said the Baron with an air of satisfaction, quite recovered from his earlier shock.

'I am almost certain your former ward is in love with Gabrielle.'

'Aha! I understand your meaning. Are you jealous? Good, that is a good sign.'

'I am certain that what I have told you is true. I shall even confess to you that one of the reasons I felt compelled to take the course of action that caused you such great sorrow was the prospect of becoming an old maid and seeing Gabrielle, seven years my junior, married before me.'

'You are right, my child,' replied the good Baron. 'This would be most unnatural, and I shall not allow it. I give you my word as a Charassin that Monsieur de Vaudrey shall have you, and not Gabrielle, as his bride. But you seem to have forgotten that a marriage is founded on more than just love. Do you promise to put your faith in me, and, should I prove successful in my negotiations, do you give me your word, little Miss Henriette de Charassin, that you will accept Paul's offer of marriage?'

'How dear you are to me, Father!' cried Henriette, kissing his white hair affectionately. 'There is nothing I would not do to make you happy. You have my word.'

'Sweet angel,' replied Monsieur de Charassin, pulling her close to him.

Henriette left her father's bedroom in a state of triumph and climbed the stairs to her own room.

VI

Once alone, Monsieur de Charassin returned to his armchair. Perhaps for the first time in his life, half an hour's careful reflection led to a firm resolution to act. A threat to the bloodline was all that was needed for him to take decisive action, even when it came to as delicate and complex a topic as marriage.

'Heaven and earth!' he thought to himself once Henriette had left him. 'The girl would have allowed one love affair to put the bloodline in jeopardy, but this will soon be put right. She is twenty-five years old with Spanish blood in her veins, and her head is filled with thoughts of passion. She must be married to Monsieur de Vaudrey as soon as possible, before she commits any further acts of folly. And yet, am I right to give preference to the eldest to the detriment of the others? Certainly I am, for this is a matter of family honour. And besides, Renée and Gabrielle are of Germanic stock; their temperaments will remain calm and balanced for some time. It is settled, then, I shall speak with my ward today. If he truly does prefer Gabrielle to Henriette, a nice dowry of twenty thousand francs should help him to change his mind; and if that does not suffice I shall tell him that Gabrielle is far too young for me to think of allowing her to leave home.'

Whilst we wait for the Baron to meet his ward, let us return our attention to the three sisters.

Henriette gazed at her reflection in her bedroom mirror and, finding herself rather beautiful, began to dress herself for the day with all the care and precision of one who wishes to be preferred over a rival. She could easily predict the means that her father would employ to persuade Monsieur de Vaudrey to ask for her hand and as she felt certain that Paul's love for Renée or for Gabrielle was not so profound as to blind him to the advantages of a large fortune, she awaited the outcome of her father's efforts with quiet confidence.

As she was leaving her bedroom, she saw that she had not burned Joseph's last letter to her and promptly tore it into pieces.

But it was too late: when Henriette had gone to seek out her father, Renée had crept into her older sister's bedroom, determined to establish the reason for her nocturnal excursion to the garden. Surprised to find the bedroom empty, her eyes searched the room and she caught sight of a crumpled piece of paper lying by the door. She read the strange missive from Henriette's lover in dazed shock. She blushed on behalf of her sister, dropped the letter and fled as though she had just committed a crime. However, she decided to say nothing of her discovery to her younger sister for fear that such a revelation would leave a mark on the still innocent soul of the child.

Gabrielle had been awake until dawn and slept late. Her poor head was rested. When she saw the sun shining through her curtains her heart filled with hope; she opened all the windows in her bedroom and felt renewed and comforted by the fresh air and the chatter of the birds in the trees, who seemed to be singing of love and happiness. She believed that she too was destined to be happy and loved and set about dressing herself for the day, curling her hair with her fingers and admiring her dimpled cheeks in the mirror. She selected a dress of delicate pink muslin and fastened a loose belt around her slender and supple waist, before running down to the garden. This exuberant young girl was brimming with life that morning; her lips were full and red and her skin translucent. However, her glassy eyes and febrile expression combined with sudden energetic flurries of movement betrayed a state of nervous excitement that would not be long contained and would surely bring some kind of violent reaction.

She visited every corner of the garden, but Monsieur de Vaudrey was nowhere to be found. She sat on the fateful bench and savoured her recollections of the previous evening. After some time had passed, she returned to her bedroom to finish her *toilette*, her heart heavy with the knowledge that Paul had surely grown indifferent to her. Her hope had all but evaporated and she was beginning to feel overwhelmed by a sense of impending disappointment.

Monsieur de Vaudrey had in fact gone out for the day and did not return until early evening. Upon his return, he found himself in the company of all three sisters at once and was equally gallant towards each of them. Around five o'clock, the Baron asked his former pupil to take a turn with him around the grounds. The girls intuited from the Baron's grave tone that this conversation would influence and perhaps even decide the course of their destinies.

At last the bell rang for supper, signalling the end of the torturous waiting period. They sat down at the table in tense silence. Only Monsieur de Charassin kept his irrepressible good humour.

None of the diners were able to conceal their surprise when at the end of the meal Monsieur de Charassin took Henriette's arm and led her into the Chambre Rouge, indicating to the others that they should follow.

One of the old nobleman's many idiosyncrasies was his dogged adherence to antiquated customs, and since the day that Henri IV had so famously enjoyed the hospitality of the Vautravers clan in 1595, every significant event had taken place in the Chambre Rouge, underneath the full-length portrait of the Bourbon king.

Standing under this imposing work, Monsieur de Charassin made a lengthy speech on this most moving of ancestral traditions, letting it be known that they were about to bear witness to an event that brought new joy to his old heart. He took the hands of Henriette and Monsieur de Vaudrey and, when he had asked them if they would indeed accept each other as husband and wife, ended with a typically pompous sentiment.

'I wish you both every happiness, and may the great king watch over you and grant you celestial protection.'

The Baron beamed with satisfaction, and announced that the ceremony was complete. It seemed to him that he had never been so worthy of his noble line as on this day, and his small blue eyes watered under their wrinkled lids as they had on his own wedding days.

Henriette had won. In spite of himself, Monsieur de Vaudrey could not conceal a hint of disdain beneath his affected good humour, revealing his profound indifference to Henriette.

Renée demonstrated heroic stoicism in the face of the annihilation of her happiness. She looked up as if to indicate her resignation to the heavens and as she did so, her eyes landed on the lettering on the beams that read 'Hope deceives'. These words had surely been written by one suffering from a broken heart and she found solace in this sentiment so clearly shared across the centuries. As the party left the room she looked around and noticed her younger sister sitting immobile in an armchair. When Gabrielle did not respond to her name, Renée hurried over to her and saw that she had fainted and was utterly unconscious.

'My poor sister!' cried Renée. 'She must have been more in love than I!'

When Gabrielle regained consciousness, she was completely delirious. Her speech was muddled and feverish; she revealed her secret to her sister and although it was hard to make sense of her words Renée came to understand the depth and fervour of her attachment. At last, around midnight, Gabrielle managed to fall asleep. Renée remained by her side and gazed pityingly at her sister's delicate features, somehow rendered yet more beautiful by the flush of her cheeks. She smiled in her sleep. Suddenly, in one of those rare moments of pure intuition, with the kind of clairvoyance that is possessed by only a small number of very gifted people, Renée knew that the life of this beautiful and naive creature would be filled with suffering. She tried to imagine what exactly could be in store for her sister, but as soon as she tried to focus her mind on her premonition, it dissipated entirely. However, a dark presentiment weighed on her soul, and her tears fell on to her sister's sleeping face. As though she could sense Renée's sadness, Gabrielle's expression changed suddenly and tears began to trickle from her closed eyelids.

In that moment, Renée felt a maternal urge to protect her sister. They had both been disappointed in love, and she felt the bond between them grow yet stronger because of this shared misfortune. She resolved to dedicate the rest of her life to doing all that she could to ensure her sister's happiness.

When Gabrielle awoke, she was no longer delirious. Renée questioned her and the poor child explained the story in full. She recounted the exchange on the bench, her raised hopes and her bitter disappointment, her voice so thick with pure emotion that Renée feared she would never recover. She searched her mind for some means of alleviating her sister's suffering, and devised a plan to prevent Henriette's marriage.

The following day was the day that Joseph Duthiou had demanded a rendezvous with Henriette. Gabrielle had sunk into a kind of stupor and had not left her bedroom that day.

Renée carried out her plan that very evening. However, as she was not certain that this attempt would achieve the desired outcome, and as she feared the impact of a second disappointment on her convalescing patient, she decided not to share her intentions with Gabrielle, limiting herself to some words of comfort. She excused herself from the dinner table under the pretext of tending to her younger sister and returned to her own bedroom.

She hesitated for some time before putting her plan into action. Would such actions not weigh heavily on her delicate conscience? But Henriette seemed to her so unworthy of Monsieur de Vaudrey's love and Gabrielle's unhappiness was so great that she strengthened her resolve and composed a note to Monsieur de Vaudrey that read as follows:

This evening, between ten and eleven o'clock I shall knock three times at your door. You will descend the tower stairs as quietly as possible and meet me in the garden. I have something to show you that is of the utmost importance.

Renée

When she was certain that Monsieur de Vaudrey had returned to his room, she had a chambermaid convey the letter to him. Leaving her door half open, she then blew out her candle and awaited the appointed hour with anxious impatience. When the church bells sounded at ten o'clock she heard the sound of a dress trailing on the stairs and from her vantage point behind her door she could clearly make out the shadow of her older sister moving furtively along the wall. She left her room and went to knock on the door of Monsieur de Vaudrey's bedroom. She had barely reached the bottom of the stairs when Paul appeared by her side. She took his arm and led him into the grounds by the pathway that led to the arbour.

VII

They walked in silence for some time. The moon was about to disappear behind the mountains and deprive the garden of its ethereal light. The air around them was heavy, not with dew, but with the gentle scent of the plants and flowers in the garden that wafted around them in the gentle breeze, caressing their skin as they walked. The quiet whispering of the leaves, the wistful murmurings of the river and the flowers that swayed in the night air all seemed to speak of romance; as if all of nature was languishing under the weight of desire.

Even the chaste Renée was not immune from the influence of this intoxicating atmosphere. There is nothing craven or petty about pure-hearted people; nevertheless the novelty of the situation, the task of initiating a conversation about love, no small feat for a girl of her age, and the strange nature of the secret she was about to reveal all conspired to leave her in a state of confusion, unable to speak a word.

Paul was equally overcome. Since receiving Renée's note, he had formed all manner of conjectures as to the purpose of their secret excursion, some of which were rather flattering to his vanity. He had decided that the most likely hypothesis was that Renée was in love with him and sought to persuade him to reconsider his marriage to Henriette.

When he saw her troubled expression, he felt compelled to enquire as to the motive behind this clandestine meeting. She responded in a trembling voice, 'Please, allow me to think a moment, for what I have to tell you is of such a grave nature that I am unable to control my emotion.' Paul's vanity swelled yet further. He felt Renée's arm shaking in his and he was in no doubt that this was a result of her affection for him. He felt it was his duty to apologise to her for the preference that he had shown for Henriette.

'Renée,' he said, boldly taking her hand in his, 'why have you until this moment been only cold and distant? If you only knew how I have suffered these last two days. For I know that I must be separated from you forever, I who would have dedicated my life to your happiness!'

For a moment, Renée was lost for words. However, she soon recovered herself when she comprehended the nature of Monsieur de Vaudrey's mistake.

'Monsieur,' she replied austerely, 'the state of confusion you find me in is caused by astonishment, for I cannot comprehend your conduct and I do not wish to have reason to accuse you of impropriety, so I shall not probe any further into the desires of your heart, which I believed to be loyal and loving. I did not come here to speak of myself, I came here to speak to you about Gabrielle, to whom you have also professed your love, who loves you in return, and who is currently suffering the pains of a broken heart.'

'In truth,' he replied, 'I cannot understand what I could have done to merit such censure. There has undoubtedly been a misunderstanding. Gabrielle is a charming young girl whom one cannot help but have affection for. I may even have expressed as much to her directly, but I cannot credit that such words might cause a broken heart.'

Renée was appalled by such insincerity, and promptly reminded him of the exact words he had spoken to Gabrielle: 'Tomorrow, all the world will know of our love.'

Monsieur de Vaudrey continued to feign ignorance.

'Well, Monsieur!' continued Renée. 'I shall await your reply, if indeed you have any words of apology to offer my sister, for her grief is so profound that I fear she may never recover. But first, there is something you must know about Henriette and then you may give me your response.'

They had now arrived at the arbour and Renée took Monsieur de Vaudrey aside.

'Do you see,' she whispered, 'there are two people sitting on the bench?'

The pale moon shone through the leaves, casting just enough light to identify the two figures.

Sensing Paul's hesitation, she said, 'The woman you see is Henriette, and the man sitting next to her is Joseph Duthiou, the son of a peasant. She loves him, or at least she did once. This is the woman you have chosen over Gabrielle.'

Monsieur de Vaudrey had recognised Henriette and could not deny that Renée was telling the truth. He had to admit that apprehending his fiancée in a secret rendezvous with a villager provoked in him a profound disgust, but this same woman was also surrounded by a halo worth no less than two hundred thousand francs. Greed overcame all other sentiments and with remarkable presence of mind he thought of a means to turn this most disagreeable discovery to his great advantage. He turned to face Renée, who was becoming increasingly concerned by his silence.

'Well! Since you already know what I was reluctant to reveal to you, you will be able to exonerate me as far as Gabrielle is concerned. I was already aware of Henriette's most unfortunate liaison with this man; your father himself told me of it. I am marrying Henriette to protect her from the disastrous consequences of such a lowly connection, and to preserve the honour of your family name. For Monsieur de Charassin helped my father in his time of need, and I believe it my duty to ensure that debt is repaid.'

Generosity had always been the way to Renée's heart and she did not for a moment suspect that Monsieur de Vaudrey could be trying to deceive her. She took his hand in hers.

'Paul, please forgive me for having misjudged you so gravely. You are truly a kind and noble soul.'

When they stepped out from their hiding place a few startled birds nesting in the foliage of the arbour fluttered their wings, causing a rustling sound in the leaves. The noise was heard by Henriette and her lover and they turned around to see two shadows hurrying away from them.

It had not been easy for Henriette to calm the temper of her jealous lover.

'I implored my father to give us his consent,' she had said to him, 'but even my tears were unable to move him. Now I am being watched and I dare not meet you; I do not even dare come to the garden to collect your letters. How can you speak to me thus, when I have shown you such devotion and proved my love to you time and again? I believe it would be prudent for us to separate for a short time, until the storm has passed. My father has spoken of offering you employment in his mountain property. Accept his offer, my dear, and believe that I will remain faithful to you.'

However, Joseph remained incredulous and Henriette was starting to fear he was not to be persuaded, when Renée and Paul emerged from behind the foliage.

Henriette recognised the pair immediately. Jealousy clawed at her heart at the sight of them together, but she soon recovered herself and, with the sang-froid that is inherent to deceitful people, thought of a means to regain control of the situation.

'Do you recognise these two, Joseph?' she cried. 'Will you still claim that Monsieur de Vaudrey is in love with me? Can you not see that he clearly loves Renée? Why else would they be together at this hour?'

Joseph grudgingly acquiesced, but was not entirely convinced. For this evening he had found Henriette, who had barely been able to hide her disdain for him, to be quite cold despite her protestations of loyalty. He withdrew, already plotting his revenge in the event that his suspicions were confirmed.

Henriette was anxious for her lover to leave so that she could rejoin Paul and Renée and enjoy their discomfort at having been apprehended. She did not for a moment suspect that it was in fact she who had been caught. She quickened her pace and soon reached them.

'Whatever could you be doing in the gardens at this hour?' she asked them, fixing Renée with a threatening stare.

'My dear Henriette,' replied Monsieur de Vaudrey with a sneer, 'perhaps you will allow the motive for our nocturnal rendezvous to remain unknown. Did we demand that you reveal exactly who it was you were speaking with earlier and what the purpose of his visit could have been? On the contrary, we moved away as discreetly as the circumstances would allow, utterly convinced that any Charassin girl would be incapable of doing or saying anything that might contravene the laws of honour and duty.'

Henriette looked at them in petrified silence, before collecting herself sufficiently to throw her sister a look of pure hatred, for she was certain that Renée had either arranged to meet Monsieur de Vaudrey that night with the sole intention of confessing her love for him, or had learned of her older sister's secret and conspired to lead her fiancé to the scene to catch her with Joseph.

The three of them returned to the castle together, breaking the silence only to comment on what a lovely evening it was, how warm the air and how clear the sky.

'One of those Italian nights, when lovers meet in secret at midnight,' said Paul sarcastically.

'A beautiful night like this can contain suffering as well as love,' replied Renée.

'In a clear sky, the moon and stars can shine a light on betrayal and vengeance,' Henriette added.

They had reached the chateau. The group bade one another good night and went their separate ways.

Before returning to her bedroom, Renée slipped into Gabrielle's bedroom and found her fast asleep. She sat for some time, looking at her with tenderness and pity.

'My poor sister! Would that I could suffer for both of us! Will she be able to comprehend the demands of family duty? At least she still has me, who will endeavour to ease her suffering.'

VIII

Eight days passed, over the course of which Gabrielle's health appeared to improve, but her suffering had undeniably left its mark on her delicate and impressionable soul. Her moods became increasingly unpredictable; sometimes she gave herself up to sorrowful daydreams, at others she was seized by feverish euphoria that recalled happier days when her expression had not been mournful and downcast. Her gaze would often fall on Paul and she would fix him with a stare that contained as much disgust as it did longing.

These looks only flattered the vanity of their object, who took this aversion to be proof of her strong feelings for him. Renée alone understood the dangerous state of mind that possessed her younger sister. Their father had not even noticed the change in her temperament, let alone understood the cause of it.

Following the advice of his eldest daughter, the good nobleman had offered Joseph work that would keep him out of Domblans for a few months. On that score at least Henriette could have some peace of mind, but she could not help but feel that Paul's flawless manners towards her were sometimes tinged with a hint of disdain. However, she hoped that her fiancé's mood would soon improve and, as the wedding date had been agreed for the following month, she diverted all her energy and attention into preparing her dress and train.

One morning Monsieur de Charassin came to find his daughters and Monsieur de Vaudrey as they were taking a turn around the grounds. He was holding a letter in his hand, beaming widely.

'I bring the most wonderful news, my daughters. Monsieur de Morges, whom I served with in the army and count amongst my dearest friends, is to pay me a visit. He says he will arrive tomorrow.'

He then took his future son-in-law aside and began a lengthy explanation of the Morges family line, interspersed with memories of their younger days when Morges was in his gallant and chivalrous prime.

'He was a six-foot beast of a man, who could have seen off an army of jealous rivals and cuckolded husbands with a mere glance.'

Monsieur de Morges arrived the following day. He was a man of around fifty years of age. His stature was certainly impressive, although he seemed to have to lean the upper part of his body backwards to maintain his balance, thanks to the prominence of his middle. He had a ruddy complexion, and thin purple veins stood out on his nose and cheeks. Although he was long past his prime, he had clearly been handsome in his day, in that vacuous inexpressive way that is often found in the noble classes. On the crown of his head there was a handful of grey hair and his heavily lidded eyes had a bawdy leer that hinted at a lecherous nature. Monsieur de Morges was a wealthy man and his demeanour suggested the arrogance of a financier, the disdain of a gentleman and the ruthlessness of a soldier.

A small and delicate man himself, Monsieur de Charassin had a profound respect for tall, well-built men, thus Monsieur de Morges represented his masculine ideal. Blinded by friendship, he still saw his friend as he had been thirty years ago, a hero of the king's guard.

On the day of Monsieur de Morges's arrival, Gabrielle was seized by one of her bouts of nervous joy that briefly restored some of her former liveliness and bright complexion. Every now and again her tired eyes would sparkle with febrile energy that hinted at a vivacious, magnetic personality. Monsieur de Morges was utterly captivated. He liked to think that he had a certain way with women and was extremely taken with Gabrielle's beauty. He had dedicated much of his leisurely existence to gallantry but this second-rate garrison Casanova found himself quite helpless before the naive charms of the young girl and fell hopelessly in love with her.

After several sleepless nights, which remarkably brought no pallor to his ruddy cheeks, nor had any noticeable impact on his considerable girth, Monsieur de Morges decided that his bachelor days were coming to an end and it was time to add the name of his beloved Gabrielle de Charassin to the de Morges family tree. Having resolved to return to reside in his ancestral seat, he relished the prospect of having this beautiful young girl as a companion to enliven the long, lonely days and distract him from the gout and other aches and pains with which old age had begun to afflict him. He confessed his feelings to the Baron and asked him for his youngest daughter's hand.

'It may be said that I am no longer in the first flush of youth,' he said to his old friend, 'but you are surely aware of my fortune of sixty thousand livres a year, and of course you know I will not accept a dowry. Moreover, in these regrettable days when noble blood is so often tainted through an unfortunate marriage, is it not the duty of those who have preserved the integrity of their bloodlines to unite and ensure the survival of the true nobility, pure and untainted by bourgeois blood?'

'My dear friend,' replied the Baron, taking his hand and shaking it energetically, 'must we stand on ceremony in this way? Is the bond of friendship that ties us not reason enough for me to wholeheartedly grant you my daughter's hand?'

In spite of this warm acquiescence, Monsieur de Morges felt the hopeful fear of a prospective lover and for the first time in his life doubted the power of his own charms.

'But do you think Gabrielle would consent to marry me, when I am thirty years her senior?'

'Heaven and earth!' cried the Baron. 'How could she possibly refuse? It would be most illogical to do so. Refuse a handsome, wealthy noble suitor who, what is more, adores her? Rest assured, my dear friend, you have nothing to fear. I shall take care of everything. It is clear that you are not familiar with our provincial ways; these are innocent young girls who know nothing of love and who, once they are married, will become dutiful and virtuous wives who will dedicate themselves to the happiness of their husband and children. What is more, Gabrielle is a particularly naive and impressionable young thing. You will see, no one understands my daughters better than me and I command their complete respect. I therefore grant you both my consent and that of my youngest daughter. However,' he added, 'you will do me the honour of ensuring that although she is by no means the first woman to turn your head, she will certainly be the last.'

'You have nothing to worry about on that score,' replied Monsieur de Morges with the self-satisfied smile of an ageing Casanova. 'Never before have I been so captivated by any woman.'

Thus the marriage was agreed between the two old friends. Monsieur de Charassin was delighted to be able to repair the injustice he had done his two youngest daughters by giving Henriette such a large dowry, and so did not hesitate to sacrifice Gabrielle to a man thirty years her senior, surely condemning her to a life of solitude with someone who was not in the least capable of satisfying the demands of her young heart.

The following morning, Monsieur de Charassin sent for Gabrielle.

'Take a seat, my child,' said the Baron. 'I have a serious matter to discuss with you, but first you must reveal your heart to me as though I were your closest friend. Tell me, what is your opinion of Monsieur de Morges?'

'Monsieur de Morges?' replied Gabrielle, quite taken aback. 'Truthfully, Papa, I do not know how I should answer you, for I have barely thought of him.'

'Come, my child, do not be shy, for it is your happiness that we are considering. Please, speak openly and tell me all your feelings about my old friend.'

'Because it is you who have asked this of me, Father, I shall obey. I find Monsieur de Morges red-faced and rather overweight. His voice is so disagreeable that the mere sound of it causes me to shudder. What is more, he rarely addresses me directly, but instead sits next to me sighing so loudly the whole village can probably hear him. Since his arrival I have not ceased to find his presence most importunate, so often does he seek me out when I wish to be alone. In sum, I find him both overbearing and unbearable,' she added with malice, hoping to raise a smile from her father whose expression darkened with every word she said.

But Monsieur de Charassin's disappointment had rather ruined his appetite for levity.

'Gabrielle,' he said sharply, 'you seem to have forgotten that Monsieur de Morges is a very dear friend of mine.'

'But, Father, I only spoke so because you asked me to.'

'Well, I shall tell you why Monsieur de Morges is so eager to be in your presence and perhaps you will find him less overbearing and unbearable, as you say. Monsieur de Morges is in love with you. He has done us the honour of asking for your hand and I have all but given your consent.'

'Me, marry Monsieur de Morges! He has asked for my hand!' Gabrielle cried out in shock. 'He is old enough to be my grandfather!'

'I do not find his age to be an obstacle,' replied the Baron. 'With his wisdom and knowledge of the world he will be able to better protect you from the dangers of the world. Moreover, he possesses a large fortune and comes from a noble line. It is my dearest wish to see you married to him and I trust, my child, that you do not wish to displease or disobey me.'

'And yet, Father, I must refuse,' said Gabrielle firmly.

'Choose your words wisely, my girl. A child who has been brought up well must never contradict the will of her parents.'

'I am aware of my duty to obey your word, Father, but a promise to God is more sacred even than that, and I have made a promise never to marry.'

'And may I ask why, young miss, you have undertaken to make promises of this nature without telling your father? Perhaps you could at least enlighten me as to what could have inspired you to take such a preposterous step?'

'The reason must remain a secret,' answered Gabrielle calmly. 'However, out of respect for you I shall reveal it. I love a man whom I cannot marry.'

This revelation left the poor Baron in utter shock. Fearful that any further enquiry would reveal that there was yet another peasant involved in this intrigue, he decided that he was unable to suffer through such a confession a second time and refrained from pressing Gabrielle on the matter. He hoped that the reaction that had proved so effective in Henriette's case might bend her will, and so began to reproach, threaten and curse her but Gabrielle was resolute. However, when he resorted to pitiful begging, the young girl softened and asked for some time to consider his request.

After leaving her father, Gabrielle ran to her bedroom and locked the door and remained there until evening in a feverish and perplexed state. Her heart was racked by painful indecision. Her father's proposition had overturned all the ideas she had formed for herself about love and destroyed her most precious fantasies. Was her father not asking her to violently reject all of her morals? If she agreed to this marriage, was she not renouncing all hope of love and happiness?

From the depths of her despair she concocted a delirious plan. Before making her decision, she resolved to meet one last time with Monsieur de Vaudrey. The following day she sought him out and asked him to walk with her around the grounds. When they reached the bench where just a few weeks earlier they had confessed their love for one another, she sat down and gestured for him to take his place next to her.

'Paul,' she said in a trembling voice, 'do you remember telling me here, in this exact place, that you loved me?'

'Is it not now our mutual duty to forget the past?' replied Monsieur de Vaudrey.

'Forget?' cried the young girl with bitterness in her voice. 'Are you able to forget? You never loved me; I have always known it to be true!'

The young girl hid her face in her hands.

'I am innocent of these accusations,' said Paul in a tone of gentle reproach, fixing her with an expression that begged her forgiveness.

In the face of such obvious suffering, the conceited fool continued to play with the young girl's heart.

Monsieur de Vaudrey's tone and expression left the young girl unsure what to make of his reaction. She said nothing for several moments, then burst into tears.

'But, Paul!' she cried. 'I do not mean to accuse you; I am the only one at fault here, for not being able to make you love me as I love you.'

'Has Renée not disclosed to you the reasons for my actions and that they are born of duty and gratitude alone?' he asked.

'Renée has hidden nothing from me,' Gabrielle sobbed. 'But if you loved me as I love you, you would have sacrificed duty, gratitude, even honour for our love.'

At this, Monsieur de Vaudrey could not stop himself from smiling.

'Gabrielle, my child, you do not know the world as I do, and you still understand things according to the laws of your own heart. Do not harbour any regrets, my young friend; believe me, there will be plenty of time for that. Your father has told me of Monsieur de Morges and his proposal of marriage. I advise you from the bottom of my heart to accept his offer, for Monsieur de Morges appears to possess all the qualities of an excellent husband and will be able to guarantee your happiness.'

'Happiness!' Gabrielle cried out bitterly. 'There is no more happiness for me! I was happy for one day and one day alone, when you held my hand in yours and kissed my forehead and promised to ask for my hand. That day I was able to see a future for myself; I was in love and believed that I was loved in return.' Her voice rising as she spoke, she added, 'If you had returned my love, I would have found the strength to stand up to my father; I would have braved his anger. You may be able to marry someone else, but I would have remained faithful to you. My feelings were powerful enough to last a lifetime, I am sure of it.'

Monsieur de Vaudrey was a little disturbed by this vehemence that contained more than a hint of madness, and for the first time felt some remorse for his conduct. What could he now say to restore this poor young thing to her senses? He made some vague consolatory gestures in the vain hope that this might help matters.

'One last question,' she sobbed, 'do you love her?'

'Who?' asked Monsieur de Vaudrey.

'Henriette.'

'Is it not my duty to love her? And must I not love you as I would a cherished sister?' he replied.

For a moment Gabrielle was unable to speak.

'Of course! You are right, of course! And you shall never hear from me again. Adieu!' she cried, attempting to gather her strength and leave him. However, before she was fully upright she collapsed back on to the bench, trembling and pale.

The following day Gabrielle did not leave her room, claiming a migraine. For she truly was sick, and Renée's loving attention and gentle consolations could not cure her.

Paul did not love her. What now was the purpose of her existence? At some moments she felt as though she were going mad. When she sat at her window watching the gentle flow of the river beneath her, the slow, monotonous movement of the water seemed to be inviting her to throw herself into its current and be carried far away.

That evening, her father visited her in her bedroom. He recommenced his campaign and, in her weakened state, the young girl gave her consent.

However, as soon as she had given her word, her aversion to the man revived with an even greater intensity. She felt as though she had been locked in a tomb and left for dead. Gripped by a sudden survival instinct, she resolved to retract this promise that had been extorted from her in a moment of supreme weakness. She would find a way to resist her father's command; he had no right to order her to sacrifice all hope of happiness in her life.

When she caught sight of Monsieur de Morges walking in the garden the following day, she decided to speak to him. As soon as he saw her, he hurried towards her, thanking her profusely for accepting her father's request. Gabrielle looked down in embarrassment but Monsieur de Morges took this reaction as modesty.

'I would like to speak with you, Monsieur,' she said.

'I am all yours, my dear,' he answered, offering her his arm.

They walked for a few moments in silence. Gabrielle tried to find the courage to start the conversation.

'You need not be so modest, my angel,' said Monsieur de Morges, noticing her distress. 'You may speak to me as you would to your best friend. What is there to be afraid of? Surely you must know by now that I adore you.'

'Let us sit in the shade of this tree,' said Gabrielle, hoping that she might feel more courageous under the cover of the foliage.

When they were seated on the bench, Monsieur de Morges took her hand. She recoiled in shock.

'Must I wait a little longer for this hand to belong to me?' he asked.

'Indeed,' replied Gabrielle in a low voice. 'That is precisely the reason I wish to speak with you.'

She fell silent once again.

'Please, speak your mind. Do not leave me to suffer the torture of uncertainty. Your father informed me last night that you had given your consent.'

'And today I wish to retract it,' said Gabrielle, her voice trembling.

'What could have happened to change your mind? Whatever obstacles there may be, I assure you that my love is strong enough to overcome it.'

The young girl looked at the ground and said nothing.

'Please, speak! Tell me what is in your heart,' begged the despairing lover, a note of panic in his voice. 'Perhaps the mere sight of me repulses you. If this is the case, I am truly cursed for I love you as I have never loved before.'

Gabrielle knew from experience the pain of unrequited love, and her reply was gentle.

'You do not repulse me, dear man. But I cannot love you.'

'If you do not hate me, then I beg you, allow me to live in hope,' he cried out, falling to his knees before her. 'I have never been so foolish as to assume that you love me as I do you, but, Gabrielle, I promise to devote myself entirely to your happiness, so that one day you will understand the depth of my affection and learn to love me in return.'

The idea that she could one day come to love this man horrified the young girl, yet she was simultaneously moved by such a sincere declaration of feeling.

'He must truly love me,' she thought to herself.

She was still thinking of an appropriate response when she noticed that tears had started to run down his cheeks. Passion and suffering seemed to transform his features, and Gabrielle was overwhelmed by sympathy.

'Let it be so! I shall accept your proposal,' she said.

She stood up and walked away, leaving Monsieur de Morges still kneeling in front of the bench. When she was some distance away, she turned around to see him in a most ridiculous position, trying in vain to pull himself up from the ground. She was seized by a fit of hysterical laughter. She ran to Renée's bedroom, and fell into her arms, unable to stop laughing. All of a sudden, the laughter turned into stifled sobs. Renée stroked her sister's head until the crying ceased and Gabrielle had calmed down enough to recount how she had just become engaged to Monsieur de Morges.

'But why would you consent to an arrangement that causes you so much sorrow?' Renée asked her.

'What does it matter? Paul does not love me,' replied Gabrielle, her voice heavy with a resignation Renée had not heard before.

Nonetheless, Renée hoped that the marriage would help her sister forget about her disappointed hopes and erase the memory of Monsieur de Vaudrey.

IX

It was decided that Henriette and Gabrielle would be married on the same day. Preparations for the ceremony were carried out in haste.

The whole family arrived in Besançon to pay their respects. Henriette thought of nothing but her train, while Gabrielle felt bewildered by the preparations taking place around her and left Renée to take care of her wedding dress.

The day of the marriage was upon them. With glacial indifference, Gabrielle let Renée dress her. She was as pale as the orange blossoms woven into her hair. Blue shadows under her eyes betrayed her lack of sleep. She tucked a wilted bud into her bouquet. This flower had become a symbol of her grief, as Monsieur de Vaudrey had given it to her one day as they walked in the garden.

When they were ready, the two young brides came down to greet the guests. Henriette looked radiant with happiness, in striking contrast to the pale and downcast Gabrielle. Monsieur de Vaudrey had all the indifference of a businessman who had come to sign a contract. Monsieur de Morges had turned an even deeper shade of puce, although it was unclear whether this was due to his feelings for Gabrielle or his ill-fitting new clothes. Monsieur de Charassin, for his part, demonstrated his remarkable capacity to be utterly himself, no matter the occasion. He darted from place to place with a juvenile excitement, stopping to make a comment here, and a joke there, deploying his entirely superficial charm as he saw fit.

The civil ceremony was held in the chateau and the marriage contracts were signed in the Chambre Rouge. As the wedding party was preparing to leave for the church, Henriette was handed a letter that she tore open immediately. The contents of the letter were as below.

Mademoiselle,

I now know that I have been gravely deceived by you and that you are to marry another man. I am writing to warn you that this is not the last you will hear from me. You will soon see that I will not be insulted in this way without seeking revenge.

Until we speak again,
Joseph Duthiou

Henriette was sufficiently acquainted with Joseph's impulsive nature for this threat to fill her with forebodings. She slipped the letter into her dress calmly enough, but she had turned as pale as her sister. She feared that her lover would not wait long to cause a scandal.

Her heart lightened as the carriage bearing her and her husband drew closer to the de Vaudrey residence. Monsieur de Morges and Gabrielle travelled in a second carriage. Gabrielle was utterly despondent and wore the expression of one whose heart has been so deeply broken that there seems to be no hope of future happiness.

Thus, Renée was left alone with her father in the mournful silence of the chateau that had so recently been filled with voices and laughter. While Monsieur de Charassin went to receive the congratulations of his neighbours on the marriage of his two daughters, Renée reflected on the events of the day, weeping over the fate of her younger sister. She wept also for herself for she too had lost her first love, a love that would live on in the furthest reaches of her heart.

X

The dénouement is undeniably the most difficult part of a novel. According to the rules of the art form, the dénouement must contain the pivotal moment upon which the entire edifice of the narrative is founded. It must also be a meeting point for all the elements of the intrigue. It is therefore the duty of the writer or the playwright to reserve the most dramatic scenes and moving exchanges for this part of the novel. But is this the case in real life? Are the simplest and most prosaic resolutions of works of prose and drama not also somehow the most poetic? The observant reader will notice that such endings, however commonplace they may first appear, often have the most to teach us and offer the most profound insight into the human condition. Let us, then, bring our modest tale to its quiet conclusion, and put aside the conventions of storytelling with their twists, turns and entanglements.

Two days after the departure of her sisters, Renée received a letter from Henriette, the contents of which are revealed below.

Mademoiselle,

Paul has told me the extent of your loyalty and affection for your elder sister. I now know that you conspired to betray a secret that could have ruined my prospects of marriage forever. Had Paul not been so generous, I would have fallen victim to your jealous scheming.

Monsieur de Vaudrey no longer feels anything but disdain for you. You should not be surprised to learn that we intend to break all contact with you and with Gabrielle, whose coquetry and shamelessness as far as Paul is concerned has known no limits. I have suffered so much at the hands of you and your sister over the last few years that I shall not regret this separation.

Farewell, then, forever.
Henriette

Renée could not believe the contents of this letter to be true. It did not seem possible that Monsieur de Vaudrey could have judged her conduct in such a way. Had she not been quite clear about the purpose of her actions? However, she soon consoled herself with the thought that this spiteful missive was clearly a means for Henriette to have her revenge for the incident in the garden. Moreover, she preferred breaking all contact with her sister to false cordiality.

Some time passed before she heard from Gabrielle. We have

transcribed her first letter to Renée here, as it reveals the state of mind of the unfortunate captive.

What can I tell you? How can I express any of my thoughts to you, when my soul has shattered into pieces? The only idea that remains intact is the memory of you, my dear Renée. You ask about my life in Morges, whether I am adapting to my new situation, and about the chateau that has become my new home and the character of the man who is now my husband.

Since arriving here, I have fallen into such a state of despair that I am barely able to perceive the objects around me. The chateau seems dreary and full of sadness. Is this an effect of my own grief? Whatever the cause, I long to return to Domblans, which holds so many dear memories.

Monsieur de Morges is undoubtedly a good man, but he is capricious and coarse. His manners and language were learned in the military and are entirely incompatible with my more delicate sensibilities. I find his advances importunate and tedious, sometimes even aggravating. Such a union is truly a monstrous thing. I, who formed such fantastical ideas of love and marriage, find myself utterly defeated by the odious reality. Is it not awful to think that I, who have such a generous, loving heart, am imprisoned for life with a man who inspires in me nothing but irrepressible repulsion? I now understand that I should never have agreed to be married; I ought to have resisted my father's will, but sorrow destroyed my strength and I surrendered to the despair caused by the cold-hearted words of the man I loved. I felt that from that point on nothing would be able to hurt me, that it was not possible to suffer more than I already had, but I now know that whilst physical pain fades with time, the soul has an infinite capacity for suffering. Sometimes, however, I endeavour to suppress my unhappiness and overcome my aversion to Monsieur de Morges. Such attempts are in vain; I cannot hide my disgust and violent outbursts of frustration and sadness inevitably ensue, from which I emerge broken and defeated. Now I may reveal the worst of it to you: I have committed a grave error that no wife should ever make. In a moment of desperation, I confessed to him the nature of my first love, a secret that should have remained forever buried deep in my heart.

My dear Renée, I was immediately made to regret my candour, for I shall never forget his expression of disdain and mockery as I made my confession.

'Ah, so you had a lover. This would at least explain your obvious aversion to me.'

I felt myself trembling with indignation.

'You are quite mistaken, Monsieur,' I replied. 'The man I love does not love me in return, and what is more he is married. But I still love him and shall continue to love him as long as I live.'

'Did I not acquire rights over your heart, Madame?' he

answered in a tone of jealous fury that intimidated me.

'Rights?' I asked, finding myself almost speechless with shock. 'Rights?'

Up until that moment I do not believe that I had truly understood my situation. His words suddenly made clear the reality I faced. It was as though everything around me had changed; I felt a kind of vertigo, as though I were trapped in one of those awful nightmares that cast a dark shadow across your consciousness, in which you are unable to cry for help or run away. Do you understand the meaning of this word, my innocent sister? Monsieur de Morges has rights over me; I belong to him by contract. I have been living with this realisation for the last month, and I still cannot bring myself to accept it, and you may counsel me that it is best to resign myself to this reality, but I have tried and in vain.

You have always said that duty comes first; you have always been the most virtuous of all of us. But is it possible to love someone out of duty?

Love! A word that I can neither write nor speak aloud without a shiver running through my whole body.

Love means feeling illuminated in the presence of the person you love.

Love is an obsession with the memory of your lover.

Is there anything more spontaneous or irresistible than love?

Again, I ask you, is it possible to love someone out of duty? You can only pretend to love someone in this way. Would you really counsel me to act thus, Renée? Is it possible to feign love, this divine passion that lights up your face, makes your heart beat, the passion that can bring you to life or destroy you?

Renée, I am sick, my heart is in great pain. I have changed much over this last month; you would barely recognise me. But I rejoice in this: perhaps I shall find my salvation in death. I cannot envisage any other path for myself, for I cannot comprehend a life where there is no hope of love.

When one is in love, everything seems illuminated in vivid colour, the world around us is humming with life and everything seems to have a purpose. One wishes to live forever just to experience this love.

But what sorrow when one ceases to love, or to be loved. The sky is dark, the sun pale, and life becomes a yoke that weighs upon our shoulders.

But I am overwhelmed by my own grief, and there is nothing to be done; unhappy people are utterly selfish. As long we are indulged in our sadness, we do not think of the pain we may cause to others.

Come and visit me; I have so much yet to tell you, and if I did not fear causing a scandal, and if I had enough strength to take a firm decision, I would leave Morges and this nightmarish barracks and I would come to live with you and reveal all of my suffering and my despair.

Gabrielle

XI

It is most unwise and foolish to endeavour to manipulate human emotion for one's own ends. Paul and Henriette did not take long to recognise the pitfalls of a union brought about by mutual convenience rather than mutual affection.

Not unexpectedly given what had gone before, the honeymoon period was short-lived for the newlyweds. From the moment Monsieur de Vaudrey acquired the two hundred thousand francs he had so coveted he no longer hid his disdain for his new bride, taking every opportunity to mock and denigrate her. Henriette continued to love her husband with all the obstinacy of unrequited love. However, she was proud and imperious and when she realised her love received nothing but ridicule in return, she locked it away deep in her heart, and after communicating to her new husband in a cold and distant manner that his feeling of disgust was entirely reciprocated, she ran to her bedroom, locked the door and burst into tears.

Two weeks passed. Monsieur de Vaudrey announced they would host a ball in the courtyard of the chateau to celebrate their marriage, as was the custom in the region.

The ball was attended by all the inhabitants of the surrounding area. Large crowds swarmed around a table loaded with beautiful cakes and generous pitchers of wine. The air was filled with the sound of inebriated youngsters singing bawdy ballads of the local area. Before long a mass of rather coarse-looking girls and boys were dancing wildly to the sound of two violins scraping the tune of a country dance.

In the middle of the ball, Monsieur and Madame de Vaudrey appeared at their window to greet the crowd. Henriette had surveyed the festivities with a combination of interest and horror when she suddenly caught sight of something that made her start in shock: she had seen her former lover among the revellers. To make matters worse, he had clearly also seen her and greeted her from afar with an impertinent familiarity.

She withdrew from the window and went to lock herself in her bedroom, filled with apprehension.

Later that evening, when the last sounds of the ball had died out, she dared to creep down to the garden. There she found Monsieur de Vaudrey.

'Has the ball finally finished?' she asked. 'I find these festivities excessively tiring.'

'This sumptuous celebration of our happiness is a rather unpleasant farce, would you not agree, Madame?' replied Monsieur de Vaudrey. 'Still, the world is full of such strange things.'

'Are we finally free of that intolerable crowd?' asked Henriette impatiently.

'Oh, Madame! You have become quite the aristocrat. As far as I am concerned, this is a welcome change, but what if Joseph Duthiou were to hear you speak so?'

Monsieur de Vaudrey had barely finished his sentence when a

man suddenly emerged from a nearby thicket and stood before them. Henriette could not stop herself from crying out in shock. It was Joseph Duthiou.

'Did I scare you, Madame?' he said in a tone of false concern.

Madame de Vaudrey was so taken aback that she was only able to mutter a few unintelligible words.

'Who, Monsieur, do you think you are to trespass on our property and interrupt our conversation?' asked Paul.

'Mademoiselle Henriette knew me well, is that not so, Madame? We have known each other for a very long time,' replied Joseph.

Henriette blushed and looked at the ground.

'Have you come to speak with me, Monsieur?' she asked in a low voice.

'Madame, do you know this boy? Is this why he believes that he has the right to speak to you in such a way?'

'He used to work for my father, he is—' Madame de Vaudrey began to stutter.

'It may pain you to speak my name aloud, my lady, so I shall say it for you. My name is Joseph Duthiou!' he cried in a threatening voice.

Monsieur de Vaudrey's first concern was to prevent a scandal.

'What is your business here? Have you a debt to settle?' he asked.

'Precisely,' replied Joseph Duthiou. 'I have a small debt to settle with Madame, but I wish to speak with her alone, to help refresh her memory.'

'I beg you, leave us for a moment,' said Henriette to her husband.

Paul stood aside, leaving his wife to speak with the labourer alone.

'What do you want from me, Joseph?' said Henriette in a gentle voice. 'If you have something you wish to ask me, why not write? Why did you have to make a scene in front of my husband?'

'If I had written to you, you would not have replied,' said the craftsman. 'If I had asked to see you, you would no doubt have refused to admit me. This was the only means I had of reaching you.'

'Have you come to chastise me further? I had to obey my father's wishes, my dear Joseph,' said Henriette with an air of resignation.

'My dear Joseph! My dear Joseph!' he repeated mockingly. 'So you do remember!'

'Of course I remember!' she said with false tenderness.

'Take my arm as you once did; it will help us remember those happier days and we shall be able to speak more freely.'

He stepped closer to Madame de Vaudrey to offer his arm and she could not stop herself recoiling in disgust and horror.

'My husband can see us! What must he think?' she cried.

'Ah, I can see you have become proud,' said Joseph, throwing her an angry stare. 'Now that you are known as the Comtesse de Vaudrey you look down on a simple peasant like me and you have probably forgotten all your letters in which you expressed such noble sentiments on poverty and the honour of the working class? A most worthless honour indeed, and one that I would happily surrender. If I had been lucky enough to become your husband, as you once led me to believe I would, I would have gladly spent my days strolling in the sun, my hands in my pockets, instead of daubing walls with paint. Your letters used to make me laugh, you know, and if it seemed as though I agreed with your lofty ideals it was only to please you, my lady. On the subject of your letters, this is what I have come to tell you. Instead of burning your letters, as you asked me so many times to do, I kept a number of them, the best ones in my opinion. Would you like to see them?'

'So you have come to return these letters to me?' Henriette said carefully.

'Yes, indeed,' replied Joseph, producing a thick envelope from inside his coat.

When she saw the packet of letters, Henriette's expression changed. Her eyes glittering, she reached out to take it from his hands. Joseph anticipated her movement and swiftly returned the envelope to his pocket.

'One moment, please. These letters are truly precious to me and I dare say they are worth a hefty price.'

He paused, waiting for Henriette to comprehend his meaning.

'I don't understand, explain yourself,' she said impatiently.

'This is the situation I find myself in,' said the wily craftsman. 'Since you left me, I have sought only to forget my suffering, and I have made an offer of marriage to the lovely Mélanie, the miller's daughter. She has accepted my proposal, but she is wealthy and for her father to consent I must pay five thousand francs. Now do you understand?'

'Not at all. What do you mean to say?'

'I believe I have made myself quite clear. I simply thought that, given our former friendship, you might grant me this small favour in return for your eloquent letters which mean a great deal to me as a lasting souvenir of our love, my darling Henriette. What do you think?'

'I thought such threats to be beneath you!' cried Henriette. 'I cannot believe that you are capable of such manipulation, Joseph. I truly thought you were superior to the rest of your class, that you possessed too refined a spirit to sink to such depths!'

'Refined spirits are all very well for polite conversation and turns around the garden, but they are of no practical use. Business must come first! If you feel this is beneath you, what do you say to all the lies you have told me? Is lying not also beneath you? Did you not tell me countless times, as recently as a month before your marriage, that you would never love, never marry anyone but me? These words were no more than outright lies you fed to your poor little Joseph.'

'It shall be so; you shall have your five thousand francs, but you must swear to remain silent for evermore about what happened between us.'

Joseph Duthiou's face broke into a smile.

'Five thousand francs and you have my word, not forgetting a small sum for the wedding gift. So six thousand francs in total.'

'More money!' said Henriette, struggling to contain her disgust and indignation.

However, as she found all interactions with this man odious, she agreed to his demands.

'Hand me the letters and you shall have your money either this evening or first thing tomorrow morning.'

'Oh, I do not believe I should have to wait to receive my payment,' answered the defiant labourer. 'As I said, these letters are very precious to me.'

'You go too far!' cried Henriette in exasperation. 'How dare you defy me so?'

'With such valuable bounty as I have, I believe I have every right to defy you,' replied Joseph.

Henriette had no choice but to endure these insults. She knew that she had to consent to his wishes or risk exposing herself to the most injurious scandal.

'I bid you goodnight,' said Joseph. 'I shall be staying in the village until tomorrow night. Send for me when you have the six thousand francs ready.'

They went their separate ways.

Henriette felt overwhelmed by shame and guilt and found herself in a most perplexing situation. How was she to procure six thousand francs? Could she ask her husband for the money? Would she be able to endure such humiliation? Perhaps she could ask her father? But he had already made so many sacrifices for her! Moreover, she would have to wait several days for her father's response, by which time Joseph might have demanded more money. She finally decided to ask Monsieur de Vaudrey for help.

She did not see him until they sat down for dinner that evening. They ate in tense silence, but when the servants left the dining room, Monsieur de Vaudrey addressed her in a mocking tone.

'It must be acknowledged, Madame, that I am truly a generous husband. It would, of course, be utterly beneath me to feel, and even more so to display, any jealousy towards an animal of his sort. You certainly have singular tastes, my dear. When I compare myself to that peasant, I cannot imagine how, save for a love of contrast, you can profess to have loved both myself and Joseph Duthiou.'

'Please, Monsieur, I beg you to cease your ridiculing,' said Henriette with tears in her eyes.

'What would you have me do? Am I to take such an affair seriously?'

'The man is asking for six thousand francs,' said Henriette quietly, looking down at her plate. 'That is the price he has put on his silence.'

'Six thousand francs!' Paul exclaimed. 'Is he mad or is it you who have taken leave of your senses?'

'I promised to pay him.'

'And is your father able to provide the sum?'

'I am asking you to help me.'

'You think that I would pay six thousand francs to buy your lover's silence. This is surely a joke in poor taste.'

'Is the sum too much to pay for your wife's honour?'

'What guarantee do we have that this miserable wretch will keep his word?' cried Paul in fury. 'We will be paying for his silence for the rest of our days!'

'Do I not have my dowry, Monsieur?' said Henriette, raising her head in defiance.

'You do indeed, and thankfully it is at my disposal, else we would have soon spent all of it on buying the discretion of your lovers.'

'Of my lovers?' the poor girl cried in horror.

'Madame, I can assure you I would sooner you had had ten lovers from your own class than one Joseph Duthiou.'

'You are cruel, Paul. You have already made me pay dearly for my youthful mistake these last two weeks, a mistake attributable to our lonely and isolated existence in Domblans rather than any defect in my character.'

'Which is doubtless why you now expect me to pay for it? My dear, you seem to have understood the principle of conjugal solidarity rather too literally.'

'Monsieur, have some mercy and cease your mockery. I beg

your forgiveness and implore you to do as I have asked.'

In spite of her prideful nature, Henriette fell to her knees and burst into tears.

'Spare me the theatre,' replied Monsieur de Vaudrey coldly. 'Let the man talk; nobody will believe him.'

'But he has proof,' said Henriette.

'And what might that be?'

'Letters signed by my hand.'

'How you could have stooped to such things is beyond me,' he said in a tone of utter disgust. 'As you wish, I will pay for your folly.'

Henriette looked up, so humiliated by her husband that all her love for him was replaced by pure hatred.

From that moment on, discord ruled the lives of the young couple, and each new day brought with it a similar quarrel.

A few months after his exchange with Henriette, Joseph married and came to live in the village of Vaudrey. He bought an inn and continued his extortion of Madame de Vaudrey in the most odious fashion. Aside from the letters that had cost her so dearly, he had also kept some small tokens sent by her for which he demanded a small sum. Half-finished sentences, inquisitive looks and insinuations all made their way to Monsieur and Madame de Vaudrey and provided fresh grounds for their quarrels. It was not long before tales of Henriette's former lovers turned from vague rumours to public scandal. She was forced to withdraw into complete solitude, barely able to leave her home for fear of the whispers and mocking gazes that inevitably greeted her in the village.

However, time passes and memory fades and the scandal

was slowly forgotten. Henriette's character was softened by her months of suffering. Monsieur de Vaudrey, finding little to entertain him at home, was often away for long periods. He spent increasing amounts of time hunting and abandoned his wife for the pleasures of excursions with his horses and hounds. Madame de Vaudrey felt a calm descending over her existence, although it was a barren calm, similar to that found in the polar regions. Her life was cold and colourless, devoid of the scent of flowers or the cool spring breeze, or the warmth of the sun's rays. The once passionate young woman would have preferred the poignant turbulence of suffering to this stifling and lethargic torpor.

XII

L et us now return to Gabrielle.

Five years have passed since her marriage. We find her at Domblans, in the modest little bedroom of her childhood. But it is hard to recognise in her the fresh young girl described at the beginning of this story.

Seated on a chaise longue, her pose told of her broken state. She was deathly pale, very thin and hollow-eyed. Her prominent cheekbones, pinched-looking nose and colourless lips did not at all recall the delicate features, graceful countenance or fine expression that we admired in her a few years ago. Gabrielle's sorrow was killing her. The only sign of life was in her eyes. Her intense blue gaze was sometimes magnetically powerful, sometimes alight with an extraordinary brightness, and sometimes took on an ecstatic expression as if the invalid could already glimpse the superior spheres of another existence.

Renée, good, sweet Renée, sat beside her working silently on her embroidery. A little girl of three or four was playing at her feet. The child seemed sensitive to the sadness around her, moderating her movements and taking care not to speak too loudly. Gabrielle looked at her daughter with an expression of tenderness mixed with bitterness, tears running down her face. Seeing her tears, the child threw herself at her mother, her little arms outstretched. 'Don't cry, Maman,' she implored. 'I promise I will always be good.'

Gabrielle's tears redoubled; she leaned forward and tried to raise her arms to hug her daughter close. Then her expression suddenly turned to repulsion and she flung herself backwards, pushing the child away. 'Take her away, I beg you,' she told Renée.

'Come, my child.' Renée rose to lead the child out. 'Maman wants to sleep now.'

'I won't make any noise, I want to stay,' pleaded the child, crying.

'No, come on, my angel,' insisted Renée, taking her in her arms with maternal tenderness.

The child suppressed a large sob as she was taken away.

When Renée returned, Gabrielle said to her, her voice full of tears, 'You will be a mother to her, won't you, Renée? And give her all the caresses that I cannot give her?'

'Why can you not give them? The joys of motherhood would have consoled you for all your pain, and she is still your child.'

'But she is also the child of Monsieur de Morges,' replied Gabrielle. 'And the internal conflict this causes is killing me.'

'Dear Gabrielle,' replied Renée, kneeling in front of her sister, 'if you wanted, you could still live, love your daughter and finally be happy. Make an effort, overcome your imagined sorrow. How often one sees unhappy unions, yet neither party dies!'

'My poor Renée, I can't change my character,' said Gabrielle, smiling sadly. 'Believe me, I am better off dying. If I live, I will have to return to Morges, and …'

'But why would you have to return to Morges? Your poor health is enough to explain your stay here.'

'What about Monsieur de Morges?'

'I will undertake to make sure that he sees reason.'

'Monsieur de Vaudrey won't come here,' said Gabrielle, changing the subject abruptly.

'I have heard that he had to go on a trip, and I fear he did not receive my letter,' replied Renée, looking embarrassed.

'You did write to him, you're not just humouring me?'

'I assure you I did.'

'And yet it will soon be eight days that we have waited for him. Perhaps you ought to write again and tell him that I am very ill.'

'But,' objected Renée, 'do you not worry that his visit will prove too much for you?'

'Oh no! For I have long grown accustomed to the thought of seeing him again. And you also asked Henriette to come? I don't want to die without reconciling with her, and … and I feel very weak.' Her voice was so altered Renée could barely hear her.

'Please, Gabrielle, don't say things like that, it breaks my heart.' And she covered her sister's pale hands with tears and kisses.

At that moment a carriage entered the courtyard of the chateau, and then after a few moments, voices and footsteps could be heard in the house. Gabrielle listened and as the noises drew closer, she leaned her head back on her chair and closed her eyes as if to gather her strength and contain her emotion, but soon, with the intuition that comes where great passion or an impressionable nature are involved, she murmured, 'He has not yet come.' The door opened and Monsieur de Charassin brought in Madame de Vaudrey.

Seeing Gabrielle in such a state, Henriette was momentarily stunned and filled with dread. But she promptly recovered herself, and, filled with pity and remorse, flung herself, crying, into the arms of the invalid. The three sisters, separated for so long, stayed silent for a few emotional moments, their hearts filled with tears and memories of their past together.

Henriette was also unrecognisable. The intense sorrow she had lived with for five years had hardened her features, darkened her expression and veiled her gaze. Her chin was even more prominent now and her complexion, once so delicate and pale, was now tanned and weather-beaten. Every part of her face seemed to speak of bitterness and disappointment.

'Why has Paul not come?' Gabrielle asked her. 'Would you be jealous of a dying woman?'

'Let us not speak of the past, I beg you,' said Henriette. 'I was very unjust towards you and I have come to make amends for my bad behaviour whilst it is still within my power to do so.'

'Yet I would have liked to see him,' said Gabrielle, who was determined upon it.

'Unfortunately he is travelling,' replied Henriette, after a sign from Renée.

'Yes,' the invalid went on, 'but I would have liked to see him, to tell him that I forgive him and that when I have passed on I will pray for his happiness.' After a moment of silence, she continued, 'I suffered greatly as a result of my love for him and I think that is one of the reasons I am dying. At least tell me that you are happy, my dear Henriette?'

Madame de Vaudrey buried her head in her sister's lap, restraining her violent feelings. 'No, Gabrielle, no, my dearest sister,' she said, sitting up again, 'you will not die and you will know that man; you will know how little he is worthy of your love. That revelation will at the same time be my punishment.'

She then recounted to them both the sorrows of her private life. She revealed the ruse she had used to marry Monsieur de Vaudrey and how her passion for him had been rewarded by hatred and scorn. She told them of the new humiliations he found to inflict on her each day because of the indiscretion of Joseph Duthiou. She described how Monsieur de Vaudrey, selfish and corrupt, had played with the feelings of the three sisters, and had only ever had one aim, which was to enrich himself by marrying for a dowry.

Alas! Gabrielle was in no way prepared for these revelations. Seeking to cure her sister, Henriette, in her inexperience, had not calculated the impact or measured the dose of her energetic restoration of the moral order. The poor invalid was too weak to bear such a shock without danger. The revelations, by destroying forever in her that poetry of feeling which is the very essence of certain noble souls, provoked a profound transformation in her.

By evening, she had succumbed to a high fever and delirium. The doctor was summoned in all haste. 'This crisis may save her,' he said, 'or it may kill her.'

The fever lasted a week, a week of unbearable anxiety for Henriette and Renée who kept constant watch at their sister's bedside. Finally, on the first day of the following week, there was a slight improvement. The fever came down, and the devastated family began to hope again.

Gabrielle wanted to get up, and the doctor advised against dissuading her. She wanted to be washed and dressed and they put her in a white cashmere dressing gown. 'I look like I'm getting married,' she said, smiling.

Then she asked for flowers, fresh air and sun. They brought her the most beautiful flowers from the greenhouse and she received them with childlike joy. They opened the window. It was a beautiful April day, a little chilly, but bright and invigorating. The invalid breathed in the health-giving air with a sort of sensual pleasure. 'How good it is! How good to breathe fresh air. It feels as if I am breathing in new life. No, I sense it, I will not die; besides, I want to live. Life is so good! It feels as if the last five years have been nothing but a bad dream and that I am back as I was when I was eighteen, in our dear old home, insouciant and happy like before. We will still love each other for years to come, is that not true, my sisters? And we will still be happy.'

Henriette and Renée were crying with joy. 'Don't talk so much,' they said to her, 'you will tire yourself.'

'I have so much energy today, and I can't remember the last time I felt so light-hearted. Health and happiness are returning through every pore; so allow me to tell you how well I feel. To think that a few days ago I wanted to die – I must have been mad! I'm still so young and I can become beautiful again. Renée, hand me a mirror.'

Renée rose and pretended to look for a mirror.

'I used to think,' Gabrielle went on, 'that I could not live without love. But now the important thing for me is life itself, and I dread those violent feelings that cause death. Joy and peace are to be found in friendship!'

She fell silent and appeared pensive. But then continued: 'I feel completely restored. I feel less aversion for Monsieur de Morges. Poor man! How unhappy I have made him! How unfair I have been to him! He loved me so … Renée, you must write to him and tell him to come. Tell him I would like to see him here. I want to ask his forgiveness for all the harm I have done to him. And my daughter,' she asked suddenly as if she had just remembered, 'where is she? I want to see her! Where is she? How I will love her, from now on, my dear little angel!'

At that very moment a child's footsteps could be heard on the stair. The door opened and Gabrielle's daughter entered. For several days she had been forbidden to enter Gabrielle's room; but as she had heard that her mother wanted flowers, she had come triumphantly to bring her the most beautiful rose from the greenhouse.

Seeing her child again, Gabrielle shuddered imperceptibly, and, although she was still extremely weak, she found the strength to stand up and hold out her arms. 'My daughter! My daughter!' she cried tenderly. She took the child in her arms and hugged her close, then fell, insensible, into her chair. Her sisters thought that she had fainted and hastened to help her, but Gabrielle was no more. That burst of passion had exhausted what was left of her life.

XIII

A few years ago, some business matters led me back to Domblans, the village where I was born. In general, it is better to be content with one's memories than to return after a long absence to the people and places we have held dear. Memories keep alive forever our impressions of happiness and images of beauty, whilst lessening the dark points that could mar the picture. Thus, the dear village of my memory, full of bustle and gaiety, now appeared sad and deserted. As the Charassin family had been closely linked to mine, and as I retained a great fondness for Renée, remembering her beauty as well as the exquisite goodness of her heart, I decided to pay her a visit.

I was shocked when I first entered the courtyard of the chateau. Although Renée's tender care had ensured that everything was clean and orderly, a deathly silence reigned over the dwelling so that my footsteps, as I made my way up to the porch, produced a sinister noise that frightened me.

I was shown into the grounds where I found Monsieur de Charassin with Renée. It was a pale, warm autumn day. Yellowing leaves, stirred by a melancholy breeze, were starting to cover the ground, and the sun was struggling to appear from behind clouds so grey they increased my feeling of depression.

Renée and her father hurried over to greet me. I found the Baron little changed. He possessed the kind of temperament that is only lightly touched by sorrow, because it is too shallow for pain to make an imprint in it. He was still the jovial old man I had previously known, but with a few more wrinkles and grey hairs. As for Renée, I barely recognised her. She was extremely thin and her strained expression bore witness to a strong soul which had bravely faced up to life's disappointments. Her long, remarkably noble yet serious face was of a smooth ivory complexion. The slight furrows on her brow and temples were signs that misfortune had prematurely aged her beyond her thirty years. The mysticism in her large blue eyes, often turned towards the sky, seemed to say that she had renounced happiness here on earth, and that she found consolation in the hope of another life. Mademoiselle de Charassin personified disillusionment and resignation.

Our meeting was gloomy for it evoked the memory of those who had departed. Renée took my arm and offered to take me on a walk. Our eyes and voices were full of tears. No doubt she took my silence and my glances at her as questioning because she said to me, taking me by the hand, 'Stay with us until tomorrow, and I will tell you what has happened to leave this place forever in mourning and pain.'

Foreseeing some tragedy in the story, I accepted the invitation as much out of curiosity as interest.

So that evening Renée recounted the whole story. Just as she finished, a little girl, blonde and delicate, joined us. I was struck by the already serious and melancholy expression on the child's graceful face.

'This is Gabrielle's daughter,' said Renée.

'She looks just like her!' I observed.

'I fear for her happiness,' replied Mademoiselle de Charassin, 'for she is even more like her in personality than she is in looks. She is worryingly precocious and so impressionable that I always fear that some strong emotion will break her delicate spirit. In taking on the upbringing of this child, I have, I know, assumed a great responsibility. The happiness or unhappiness of a life is almost always determined by upbringing.'

She then began a critique of education and marriage. The conversation proved to me that from the depths of her solitude, her just spirit, enlightened by the misfortunes of her family, had learned to know the world and its passions.

'After thinking for a long time,' she said, 'about the painful destinies of Henriette and Gabrielle, I am forced to conclude that they were the inevitable result of our superficial education and sheltered life in Domblans, where we could only see the world through our childish illusions. And since Monsieur de Morges has entrusted me with this child, I propose to give her an education that will, by developing her intellectual powers, protect her from her excessive sensibility, and when she is fifteen or sixteen, we will go and live in a large city where I will introduce her to the world, so that she knows how it works, and I thus hope to spare her the dangerous illusions under which girls are normally brought up. I will therefore be able, with a clear conscience, to allow her complete liberty to act as she pleases, including in affairs of the heart. I will, however, dissuade her from marriage for as long as possible, at least until she is able to know a man well enough to be sure of his character and of his love for her.

'If I were to live my life over again,' Renée went on with a sigh, 'instead of according so much importance to feelings, I would have spent much more time flirting. Since we live in such corrupt times, when men worship the golden calf above all things, using love and its delicate attentions merely to enrich themselves, a flirtatious woman who only takes from such men what they have to give, that is to say, their insincere compliments, has a chance of being happy. So, when my poor little Gabrielle reaches the age of love, I will endeavour to become young again and will teach her coquetry, in order to bolster her against the distractions of passion.'

When Mademoiselle de Charassin had finished speaking, we were both silent for a moment.

I was thinking of those three young girls, those three destinies ruined by worthless love. Was not the most unfortunate, I said to myself, Renée? Renée, whose noble, lofty spirit and generous, tender heart had been transformed by terrible disappointments; who rejected love and perfection as trickery, as a chimera. Renée, a flirt! I could barely suppress a sad smile. Her candour and innate kindness could never have stooped to coquetry and the cold calculations it required. But I did not have the strength to contradict her conclusions; I felt only admiration for her devotion and pity for her misfortune.

The rest of the evening passed in melancholy conversation, occasionally enlivened by our memories of childhood. The next morning I took my leave of Renée and the old Baron, thanking them for their kind welcome, although I was taking away many bitter thoughts.

AN ATONEMENT

I

This first scene took place at the Théâtre-Italien, near the end of winter 1850. Two young men sat in the orchestra stalls. They had surveyed the entire auditorium through their opera glasses before settling on a box near the front of the stage.

'There is the Comte de Montbarrey and the Marquise de Germigney,' said one of them.

'That is a surprise,' replied the other. 'I thought the Comtesse de Montbarrey was critically ill.'

'Not critically ill, but unwell, and very jealous too – two reasons why her husband is at the show in more pleasant company.'

'Is the Marquise not a close friend of the Comtesse?'

'And of the Comte, it seems.'

'That can't be. Monsieur de Montbarrey is no longer young, and I find him quite uncompromisingly ugly.'

'That is true, but he is thought to be a man of great passions. So, watch out for that splendid virtue!'

'Is the Marquise's virtue therefore intact?'

'Opinions are divided, but wrongly so. The Marquise does not quite have a heart of ice, because ice melts.'

'Have you perhaps experienced her icy rigour?'

'No, but one of my friends fell madly in love with her, and his folly resulted only in making the Marquise fashionable and giving her a reputation for being beautiful that, in my opinion, she is far from deserving.'

'I still think she is very beautiful.'

'I find her quite ordinary-looking, and I do not much like her red hair.'

'She has elegance and distinction.'

'Well, my dear fellow, since she has not yet chosen from amongst her numerous admirers, you might put yourself forward. She is a brilliant match; the Marquis de Germigney has left her a private income of two hundred thousand francs.'

'Truly?'

'Really, my dear friend, you are eyeing the Marquise most intently … If you would like a closer look, I will introduce you; but I warn you, do not wear your heart upon your sleeve, because the Marquise is an out-and-out coquette.'

'No, thank you! The fact that she is a coquette is not what holds me back: coquettishness is, in my opinion, the foremost of women's rights. But I do believe she is in love with the Comte de Montbarrey. They have not said one word since I started watching them, but they look at each other frequently, and there is a naive tenderness to the Marquise's gaze, like that of a young girl in love for the first time. The Comte has a twinkle in his eye. He really has a most expressive face, and I am beginning to find him less ugly.'

It was true that Béatrix de Germigney did not have the sort of dazzling beauty that captivates people straight away. She had another, more subtle beauty that was revealed by closer examination: the fine features, delicate colouring and varied expressions that charm the observer, and give the face its character, so to speak.

Madame de Germigney was twenty-four years old at the beginning of this story, but with her limpid eyes, soft skin and youthful smile, you would have thought her only twenty. Her naturally wavy hair had tones of warm mahogany, an unusual colour favoured by painters for bringing out the radiance of the complexion. The Marquise's hair, powdered with fine gold dust, was pulled back in the style of Mary, Queen of Scots, revealing her smooth, flawless brow and her perfect oval – albeit a little narrow – face.

Her well-proportioned blue eyes, framed by long golden-brown eyelashes, sloped down towards her temples, giving a tender and melancholy air to her expression. Her slightly aquiline nose with its daintily defined nostrils suggested a proud and sensitive spirit. Madame de Germigney's face was usually pale, but animated. At the slightest emotion, it was as if a light appeared behind this translucent alabaster façade, tinting it with the sweetest shades of pink. But it was her perfect waist, admired for its elegance and suppleness, that guaranteed Madame de Germigney her reputation for beauty.

That evening, the Marquise was wearing a dress made of soft purple velvet, its lace bertha fastened to the front of the bodice by a modest bouquet of Parma violets. The simplicity of her attire only added to her elegance, as the contours of her arms and neck were so flawless that any ornamentation would have spoiled their perfection and beauty.

Having had a strict upbringing, and being long accustomed to self-restraint, Madame de Germigney was dignified and aloof, with refined manners. Yet one could sometimes catch a certain brusqueness in her gestures that betrayed a once effusive nature, and when her face, normally so calm and serious, was animated by an emotion, her moist eyes shone and her nostrils and lips quivered in such a way that one could tell she had a passionate and intense spirit.

Monsieur de Montbarrey was gazing at the Marquise in silent rapture. The great clarity that love brings has always been thought of as blindness. On the contrary, love sharpens our perceptions, and reveals attractions in the loved one that go unnoticed by most. The beauty and fleeting grace to be found in the subtlest movement of the face and the slightest nuance of complexion exist for the lover only. Thus the Comte could see beyond Madame de Germigney's translucent features and into her very heart and mind.

Of all the arts, music most moves one to emotion and enthusiasm. Love and music are two pleasures that complement each other and are enhanced by the luxury and the memerising atmosphere of the theatre.

The Marquise was watching the performance contemplatively. She did not believe that she was in love with Monsieur de Montbarrey; she thought she only had feelings of friendship for him. She thought it was just her enjoyment of the music causing the unexpected languor that was making her vision hazy, the rapid shivers that were running across her entire body, and at times the sudden breathlessness that caused a tear to form upon her long golden eyelashes.

However, she felt deeply cherished, and found in this feeling of affection – which she did not analyse – a secret delight, but the Comte's passion was enveloped in so much veneration that even the most virtuous would not have been able to rebuff it. Had the sensitive Madame de Germigney suspected that this was due to love, she would have been alarmed, and would have refrained from seeing him again out of fear of stealing his affections from Madame de Montbarrey.

As far as the Comte was concerned, his passion had reached its final stage and was past remedy; it was integral to his existence, and the two of them would die together.

When the show had finished, Monsieur de Montbarrey accompanied the Marquise home, where she invited him in for tea. The carriage stopped in front of a town house on Rue de Bellechasse. They ascended a long staircase with flowers laid out along both sides, their smells and colours mingling harmoniously.

They passed through several lavish private rooms before entering an elegant boudoir draped with blue damask with a pattern of black pattern, which was held up in the corners of the apartment by a simple golden rod. The sofa and armchairs were covered with the same fabric. The rosewood furniture, which was modern and elegant and inlaid with Sèvres medallions, was a pleasant contrast to the rather dark floor of the boudoir. Four Venetian mirrors adorned the wall hanging, and on the black mantelpiece was a Louis XV clock in Sèvres porcelain and two splendid candelabras in the same style.

The Marquise sat next to the fire and indicated to the Comte the seat opposite. He seemed sad, and she could herself sense an uneasiness that she could not explain. To break the embarrassing silence, she talked about the evening, criticised the costumes of the performers and spoke at length about the music.

Despite her best efforts of imagination, the conversation petered out again. The Comte gave only monosyllabic answers and seemed engrossed in his contemplation of the fire, or in his daydreams.

'Well! Dear Comte,' said the Marquise at last, 'will you share your thoughts with me?'

Monsieur de Montbarrey winced at the question. 'My thoughts?' he replied, with a sigh.

'You seem distracted.'

He tried to smile, but a tear rolled down his cheek.

'What's wrong?' exclaimed the Marquise, who felt moved, affectionately offering him her hand.

Monsieur de Montbarrey grasped her hand and showered it with kisses, yielding to one of those sudden sensations that cause life to quicken and give thoughts an impetuous force akin to delirium. For the first time, Béatrix's heart was filled with love. She wanted to speak but the words died on her lips, and she could not summon an expression of coldness or severity. But, suddenly managing to overcome her emotion, she stood up and rang the bell. A servant appeared.

Even the strongest of emotions can be assuaged by the arrival of an outsider. The Marquise ordered tea, and, while it was being served, finished regaining her composure. Once the servant had left, she said 'My dear Comte, please forget what just happened. If you do, I will forgive you.'

Most lovers would have gallantly argued that it would be impossible to forget a moment of such happiness. But deep feelings loathe platitudes, and so the Comte remained silent.

'As for feeling anything other than friendship for you … never!' Béatrix continued firmly.

'Oh, Madame,' replied the Comte in a changed voice, 'do not insult me by believing that I could possibly think you might love me. I bowed to the force of a passion long withheld, but not to an impulse of conceitedness. My age and my ugliness forbid me to hope that you might love me.'

His answer, spoken in a plain, earnest tone, and showing no sign of wounded pride, deeply moved Madame de Germigney.

'Listen, my friend,' she said, 'I speak with complete sincerity, from the bottom of my heart. If I have rejected all your compliments until now, it is much less out of consideration for others than it is for my own peace. Illicit love affairs, which have so much appeal for some women, have always frightened me. I cannot stand the worry, the emotions, the lies that these kinds of relationships necessitate. Believe me, my friend, if you had been a bachelor, I think I would have loved you, and would have gladly entrusted you with my happiness, but I hate obstacles, I tell you, and the very idea of the problems others would cause us would be enough to destroy my love, if there were not an even more insurmountable barrier between us: my fondness for your wife.'

Béatrix spoke in a firm, sincere manner that left Monsieur de Montbarrey in no doubt as to the strength of her resolve.

'Then we must separate,' he said, in a tone that betrayed profound sorrow.

'Do you think it necessary?' replied Madame de Germigney. 'If so, let us spend some time apart. Since you cannot leave your wife in her current state of health, I will bring my departure for Italy forward a few weeks. Farewell, then,' she added sadly. 'When you are cured, write to me telling me so. Try to make it soon.'

'I fear it will be never,' he replied simply, then, with a great effort of will, he hastily left.

Madame de Germigney remained where she was for a long while, sometimes euphorically returning to the emotion she had just experienced, and sometimes fearfully pushing the memory of it away. She was more deeply in love than she dared admit, but she hoped that her affection for Madame de Montbarrey would be enough to suppress it.

II

The Comte de Montbarrey walked back to his mansion on Rue de Babylone. It was nearly one in the morning, and despite the brisk cold, he walked slowly, weighed down by a sorrow without remedy.

When he got back to the house, the servant waiting for him in the antechamber informed him that the Comtesse had asked for him several times, and had given orders for him to be requested to come to her apartment upon his return. On hearing of these instructions, which were the mark of a jealous woman, the Comte felt suddenly impatient. She now seemed an insurmountable obstacle to his love. Nonetheless, he visited the Comtesse's room. She was sleeping. He went up to her bed.

Madame de Montbarrey was barely thirty years old, but her illness had destroyed any vestige of beauty or youth in her face. However, the luxury that surrounded her indicated a desire to please. Her gaunt face was framed by a splendid lace trim, and long cuffs hung down over her bony hand, which was an unhealthy shade of yellowed ivory.

The Comte stared at her with a cold, almost cruel expression. He was silently comparing her to the seductive Marquise de

Germigney. It was as if the Comtesse could sense his gaze upon her, because her breathing grew laboured, her pale cheeks became mottled bright red and her lips began to move as she murmured unintelligible words.

'She has probably taken a sedative,' thought the Comte. And he automatically glanced at the bedside table, upon which he saw a glass and a vial. He picked up the vial to read the label and put it back on the table: it was laudanum. At that moment, the Comtesse started muttering broken sentences in her sleep.

'Gaëtan! Don't go! Stay with me! Your absence is killing me!'

'She is forcing her love upon me, even in her dreams!' he thought. 'Oh! What tyranny!' He went back to his room and sent his manservant away.

He did not go to bed, made restless by the evening's emotions. The faint light of a solitary candle illuminated the spacious apartment, with the weapons, antique furniture and dark-green wall hangings casting strange shadows upon its walls. In this quiet corner of the Saint-Germain neighbourhood, there was complete silence at this time of night. It all conspired to encourage Monsieur de Montbarrey's sombre reverie.

He walked unsteadily. At times he looked profoundly dejected, at others his face would suddenly light up. The Comte was a remarkable example of physical power combined with gentle temperament. Desire and love dominated his strong character, but his emotions were offset by his intelligence, and the strength of his passion by the goodness and moral rectitude of his soul.

His facial features were irregular and strongly pronounced. His broad forehead suggested a great richness of imagination and revealed a spirited nature, but the power and appeal of his appearance lay mainly in his gaze. His eyes could fill with captivating magnetism, or light up thrillingly. One sensed, in his highly expressive face, his quick movements and his brisk step a nervous, almost feverish sensibility that contrasted strangely with his athletic body.

The Comte de Montbarrey was about forty years old. At that age, a man who has not exhausted himself with excessive work or debauchery is at the height of his powers. Having reached his peak, he has a moment's pause in which to enjoy his faculties at their most fully developed. It is the age of great love affairs and great works of philosophy. It is as if the man rediscovers the energy and enthusiasm of his younger years; his entire body seems to revolt against decline and uses a new lease of life to delay the fatal moment. When a forty-year-old man directs his energies towards love, rather than ambition or intellectual pursuits, the youth he lacks is compensated for by his refinement and depth of passion. And when a man like the Comte de Montbarrey decides to make love the primary focus of his life, nothing can get in the way of his intensity and persistence.

The Comte continued to pace up and down, unable to stay still. He had been intoxicated by the memory of Madame de Germigney since he had left her, and, suddenly angered by his own weakness, he vehemently cried: 'Well! Béatrix, you love me! Did you not say that? Did you not demonstrate that? You love me, and we will forever be apart! And who is it that objects to our happiness? A woman withered by sickness, a woman who bores me to tears with her complaints.'

He opened the window. It was cold, the sky dark but pure and twinkling with stars. He gazed upon the myriads of worlds turning harmoniously in space.

'If unity is the principle of the universe,' he thought, 'why

119

do human passions not move, like stars, according to the laws of harmony; why is there no logic to them? Are we excluded from the divine code that presides over the universe, or is our ignorance alone to blame for the chaos that surrounds us?'

Nonetheless, the icy air cooled the Comte's burning brow and soothed the fevers of his imagination. He closed the window and found that he was a little calmer. His imagination then took another course, and he thought back to his wife's suffering.

'Have I not sometimes been cruel to her?' he thought. 'It is true that I married her even though I was not in love with her, to please my family. But, despite my coldness, did she for one second cease to lavish me with the most tender affection? And I spurned such passionate, loving tenderness; I rejected her outpourings, I hurt the delicate sensitivities of her heart. Now I am making her faded beauty almost a crime, and my indifference has probably caused this alteration to her features, this lethargic sickness that is driving her to her death. Yet it would cost me so little! A little attention, a few kind words would perhaps be enough to bring her back to happiness and health. Why seek pleasure and joy elsewhere? Why have I never taken the trouble to study and discover the charms of such a loving and devoted soul? From now on, I will try to forget Béatrix,' he added with a deep sigh. 'I will stay away from her and I will transfer all my affections to Amélie; I will do my utmost to repair the wrong that I have done to her; I will devote my life to it.'

After making these commendable resolutions, Monsieur de Montbarrey went to bed and fell into a deep sleep.

When he awoke the next day, his head felt heavy and his limbs broken. The disordered state of his bed suggested that he had had a bad, restless night's sleep. But he was greatly surprised when he noticed on the bedside table the vial of opium that he had seen in his wife's bedroom the previous evening. He tried to collect his thoughts; he very clearly remembered leaving the vial in the Comtesse's apartment. He picked it up and considered it carefully: it was indeed the same one – only, it was empty! Unable to explain this strange state of affairs and hoping for some explanation, he got up and went to his wife's room.

The Comtesse's apartment was still in darkness. The only light came from a lamp that had almost gone out, illuminating the room with a gloomy, flickering glow. The Comte went over to the bedside table, filled with a sense of foreboding. The vial was not there.

'I was not mistaken … How odd!' he murmured. Then he bent down to his wife. 'Amélie!' he said softly. And, when she did not respond, he repeated 'Amélie!' more loudly. The same silence. He took her hand. It was freezing. He shivered at the touch. He ran to the window, opened the shutters and went back to her bed. The Comtesse looked dead. Appalled, he went out and called the servants.

'Go and get Doctor Charrière!' he cried. Then he waited in a horrible state of anxiety.

The doctor arrived. He was an old man, long a devoted friend and doctor to the Comte's family. He found the Comte at his wife's bedside, mournful and still.

The doctor spent a long time examining the Comtesse's body. Monsieur de Montbarrey watched him with a look of dread. 'So, is she dead?' he asked.

The doctor did not reply. Then he carefully considered the glass left on the bedside table. 'She took laudanum,' he said, 'but where is the vial?'

The Comte winced at the question. He told the doctor, in a truthful tone that could not have been feigned, about the state in which he had found the Comtesse the previous evening, and about all the events to do with the vial of opium.

As he was speaking, the doctor seemed to suddenly remember something, but he swallowed the words he was about to say. At the same time, a terrible suspicion occurred to the Comte, filling his face with terror. Several people then entered the apartment.

'It is clear,' said Doctor Charrière loudly, 'that the Comtesse has died of a pulmonary artery rupture.'

III

Two years after the tragic event just recounted, Monsieur de Montbarrey and Madame de Germigney, now his wife, were back in the same boudoir in which the Comte had first declared his feelings to the Marquise, having been to a ball.

A year of marriage had not diminished their affection, for some close relationships are only strengthened by intimacy; there are fine spirits who can forever vary the melody of love. Constancy can either enrich or impoverish the soul.

Madame de Montbarrey was an exceptional character. In a society in which most men focused their attentions on the most banal interests, Béatrix, full of contempt for the shallow compliments lavished upon her, could only be won over by the Comte's powerful, serious passion. Happiness made her even more beautiful, because love is to beauty what the artist's final brushstroke is to a painting.

The Comte, however, even in his happiness, was preoccupied, sombre and seemed prey to a strange sense of doom. Doubt weighed upon his soul, doubt which had acquired the bitter taste of remorse.

There was sometimes such profound sadness in his eyes that

the Comtesse, deeply affected, would cry: 'Please, Gaëtan, don't look at me like that!' Béatrix could feel her husband's mental anguish, the origin of which she could not work out.

Yet at the ball they had been to that evening, Monsieur de Montbarrey had seemed even more glum than usual. The Comtesse was truly worried and resolved to question him about it.

'Gaëtan,' she said, in a voice full of emotion, 'there is sorrow in your heart, and you do not love me enough to share it with me.'

'I assure you, my dear child, that I am hiding nothing from you,' replied Monsieur de Montbarrey, in a strained voice.

'Can you promise that?' she asked, fixing her husband with a piercing look.

Gaëtan remained silent.

'Ah! You do not love me!' cried Béatrix. 'You do not love me!' She collapsed on to an armchair and cried.

Seeing his wife in tears, the Comte knew he must do everything he could to reassure her. 'Well! My dear love, I will reveal everything to you, since you insist upon it. Yes, I am suffering, and this sorrow is rooted in the very love I feel for you. I am too happy, and it seems that I was not made for such excess of happiness. I fear unhappiness, and for me, unhappiness would be losing your love. When I see you out in society, so young and so beautiful, sought after, hailed as a queen, and I think about my age and my ugliness, it seems impossible that you could love me. If I believe there is a trace of sadness on your face, I think, "Perhaps she is not happy," and I blame myself for accepting your tenderness, as if it were a crime. Finally, sometimes a terrible jealousy takes hold of me. It is ridiculous: I blush at my folly, and that is why I hesitated to tell you the reason for my suffering.'

'Oh, Gaëtan! You doubt me!' cried the Comtesse. 'It is indeed ridiculous! You are the most noble, the most tender, the best of men; I love you for these qualities, which will never grow old. Well! To spare you any reason for jealousy, we will stop going out; we will flee the whirlwind that drives us apart every evening and takes me away from you. Besides, these constant parties tire me out, and I would find no pleasure in them now, because they are for you a cause of sorrow. But no more secrets from now on. We will think out loud. Promise me, I insist upon it.'

The Comte went pale, but he promised. Béatrix noticed the colour draining from his face and felt a painful blow to the heart. 'I still do not know his secret!' she thought to herself.

She could not sleep that night, her mind racing with thousands of different theories. She was deeply upset that her husband had been keeping his thoughts from her for so long, but he was suffering; she only wanted to find out his secret so that she could share his sadness or help to cure him of it. She was lost in thought when she was disturbed by a noise coming from the Comte's bedroom. She distinctly heard him opening a window and walking around restlessly. 'Perhaps he is ill,' she thought.

Worried, she got up quietly and went into her husband's apartment. The window was still open, despite the coldness of the night. The clouds half concealed the beams of moonlight. In the faint light, Béatrix was able to make out the Comte sitting on the edge of his bed, looking like a man overcome by profound sorrow.

She went over to him, surprised that he had not heard her come in, but he did nothing to suggest that he had noticed her. Gripped with terror, she said, 'Gaëtan, Gaëtan, do you not see me? Do you not hear me? Are you suffering?'

There was no response. She tried again. Still silence.

'Gaëtan! Gaëtan!' she repeated, grasping his hand.

The Comte started at her touch. 'Ah! Is it you?' he mumbled straight away, in a strange voice.

'Why is the window open at this time of night?' she asked. 'Are you suffering?'

'Yes, I am suffering,' replied the Comte, still holding Béatrix's hand and squeezing it spasmodically. 'But what is physical suffering compared to the suffering of the soul?'

'Oh, my friend!' cried the Comtesse in a tearful voice. 'I too am suffering! I am very unhappy because I no longer have faith in your love.'

'You no longer have faith in my love, Béatrix?' asked the Comte, in a muffled voice that caused her to tremble. 'Oh, do not say that! If only you knew what this love has driven me to!'

'Well! Then tell me everything,' she interrupted. 'Evidence of your trust would make me happy. I knew you were not telling me the truth earlier; you were trying to fool me by pretending to be jealous. Speak, then, I beg you, because this restraint will kill me in the end, I can feel it.'

'Kill you, Béatrix? … But then I would be twice a murderer!'

'You are frightening me, Gaëtan. Please, explain yourself. I want you to!'

'You want me to?' repeated the Comte uncertainly.

'Yes, Gaëtan, I want you to!' said the young woman again, vigorously.

'Well! Then you will find out,' replied the Comte, as if he were yielding to an overwhelming desire. 'One evening two years ago, I had just left you, drunk on love, hopeless. An obstacle was keeping us apart … Only a crime could sweep that obstacle aside …' Then, shivering as if he had suddenly seen a ghost, he added, 'I still see this woman. She is in bed, fast asleep … I compare her to you, my beloved … to you, so young, beautiful and tender … and her, sick, faded and melancholy.'

The Comte paused for a moment. Béatrix remained motionless with dread. The Comte went on.

'I do not know how it happened, but during the night I had a kind of dizzy spell, so I got up, went to my wife's apartment and over to her bed. There was a vial of laudanum on her bedside table and I poured it into a glass. I was still uncertain; my hand was trembling. My brow was covered in cold sweat. At that moment, by misfortune, my wife half woke up. "Amélie," I said to her, "you are restless, drink this potion." I lifted her head and brought the glass to her lips. She obeyed my voice instinctively and drank what I gave her without even realising. The next day, she was dead! You see now, Béatrix, how much I loved you!'

At that moment, the moon passed between two clouds and illuminated the Comte's face. Béatrix could see his staring, glassy gaze. Trembling and distraught, she sharply snatched her hands away from her husband, let out a piercing cry and fainted.

IV

Having come round from her swoon, Béatrix was now in the grip of a raging fever. The Comte remained by her side. Pale and defeated, he seemed to be waiting for somebody in utter bewilderment.

Doctor Charrière soon arrived to examine the invalid. She was only half awake. When she heard people speaking, she opened her eyes and stared at her husband with a look of alarm. The Comte tried to take her hand, but she pushed him away in horror.

'Get out!' she cried. 'Have you come to murder me? Help! Murderer! Murderer! Amélie, watch out! It is poison … the villain! He wants to murder you so he can marry me! But I will not marry him! No, never, never!' She fell back, exhausted, muttering incomprehensibly.

The Comte seemed overwhelmed. The doctor looked at him in astonishment.

'Come into my office,' said Monsieur de Montbarrey. 'I need to talk to you.'

When they were alone, there was a silence, during which the Comte seemed to be battling a painful emotion.

'So, what happened?' asked the doctor.

The Comte did not answer. 'Do you think me an honest man?' he said, in a choked voice.

'Yes, my lord.'

'And will you be able to believe the strange things I am about to tell you?'

'I know you are honest, and I will believe you,' replied the doctor.

The Comte composed himself and began: 'Do you remember that two years ago, on the morning my first wife was found dead in her bed, the vial of opium I had spotted in her bedroom the previous night was, for some strange reason, in mine. You did not seek to explain that odd event, but doubt has weighed upon my conscience like remorse ever since, plunging me into dark, unremitting sadness. At night especially I am plagued by terrible nightmares that leave me depressed and unwell. When we returned from the ball yesterday evening, my wife begged me to tell her the reason for my suffering. I avoided her questions and left her after managing to reassure her. But what happened next? I do not understand. All I know is that around three in the morning, I woke with a start to a piercing cry. Imagine my surprise! The window was wide open, I was sitting on the edge of my bed, and my wife was lying unconscious at my feet. I hastened to pick her up and take her to her room. When she regained consciousness, she pushed me away in fright and called me a murderer, a poisoner. What did I tell her during my sleep? Doctor, can you explain this mystery?'

'Have you forgotten, my lord? You are prone to bouts of sleepwalking. At the time of the sad event you have just recalled, I fortunately remembered your mother telling me that you often experienced spells like this during your childhood. Later, these tendencies went away but they have returned due to emotional overexcitement. This is very common. So, I did not think it necessary to tell you that the Comtesse died from poisoning, because your own revelations confirmed that you were both innocent and guilty at the same time. I did not say anything, even to you, because the truth would only have made you feel needlessly guilty about an illness without a cure.'

'I am a murderer, then!' cried the Comte, hopelessly.

'Yes, but an unwitting murderer,' replied the doctor. 'I cannot hold you morally responsible for a crime committed in a dream state, when reason does not direct actions. This sad event should forever cause you regret, but not remorse, because you were completely unaware of it.'

'Even if,' continued the Comte, 'I managed to ease my conscience could Béatrix, who now knows this horrible secret, having discovered it while I was sleeping, ever forget it? Will I not always be a murderer in her eyes – the murderer of her best friend? Oh! I am so unhappy!' he cried with a sob, burying his head in his hands.

'Have hope,' the doctor went on. 'Often after a period of delirium as long as the Comtesse's, people lose all memory of what took place just before. If this does not happen, we will make her believe that you were delusional when you spoke to her.'

They went back into Béatrix's room and found her asleep. She seemed to be sleeping soundly, and her face had returned to its usual pallor.

'The fever is starting to subside,' said the doctor. 'Madame de Montbarrey's delirium will probably be over by the time she awakes. Leave me alone with her.'

When Béatrix awoke, her delirium had indeed passed. She

looked around in surprise and said: 'Where am I? What are you doing here, Monsieur Charrière? And my husband – where is he?'

'He has just left,' replied the doctor. 'He has been at your bedside since morning; your sudden turn caused him great worry.'

'So I am ill?' asked Béatrix. And her memories suddenly came rushing back: 'Ah! I remember … But it was a dream … Otherwise … But yes, Gaëtan, my husband … Send for him, please, so I can see him, so I can tell him about this absurd dream … He, who is so good! He, capable of a crime! … My God! How I have suffered! Imagine, Doctor, that it was a dream … But,' she added fearfully, sitting up and bringing her hands to her head, 'but …'

'Let us see, what were you dreaming about?' asked the doctor.

'No, no! I was not dreaming at all! Oh, it will be the death of me!' she said. She let her head fall back on to the pillow, and her eyes regained their feverish brightness.

Seeing the symptoms of the fever returning, the doctor realised he needed to be quick. 'Speak, Madame, speak,' he said, 'I beseech you, because we cannot explain the events of last night. When Monsieur de Montbarrey awoke this morning to find you unconscious by his bed, he was coming round from a terrible sleep. He remembers that he too had been completely lost in a dream, but a dream so strange and so horrible that I am afraid to tell you about it.'

'Tell me! Oh, tell me!' cried the Comtesse.

'Well! Madame, since you insist … The Comte was dreaming that his first wife had died from being poisoned, and that he was the poisoner—'

'And it was not he?' Béatrix cut in sharply, fixing Monsieur Charrière with a wild-eyed look. 'And my friend did not die from poisoning?'

'Rest assured, Madame; I have enough experience, I think, to be able to distinguish poisoning from a lung condition.'

'Yes, I was crazy!' replied Béatrix, a little calmer. 'The fever made me confused. How could I have paid attention to such a thought for even one moment? Call my husband, please; his presence will do me good.'

Obeying the Comtesse's wishes, the doctor went to the door and lifted the drapery to find the Comte leaning on the frame; pale, defeated and hardly able to hold himself up. 'Compose yourself,' he said, leading him into the neighbouring room. 'You must appear calm for the Comtesse.'

Once Monsieur de Montbarrey had calmed down, they went back to Béatrix, but the Comte could not completely hide his distress: Béatrix was struck by his paleness, his choked voice and the look of sadness on his face. Her suspicions returned.

'Was he really sleeping?' she wondered. 'Was he dreaming, as the doctor assured me? Did I not have evidence that he was awake? He squeezed my hand, he recognised me, he answered all my questions, and his eyes were wide open. What's more, his story was logical and corresponded exactly with the facts. Indeed, did I not learn of Amélie's death the day after the despairing Comte left me, never to see me again? Finally, is it not true that remorse has caused his melancholy, which all my tenderness cannot dispel? Even today, his discomfort betrayed his distress. He must have given in to a moment's impulse; to that urgent need criminals feel to confess their crimes; he must have told me everything in the hope that I would love him enough to forgive him and remain in love with him.'

Her suspicion turning to certainty once more, the Comtesse could no longer stand the sight of her husband and again dismissed him from her presence in a fit of indignation. The doctor understood the invalid's violent reaction to seeing the Comte. He had to destroy her suspicions about her husband's guilt. Only one way remained: tell her the truth. That is what he did. At first, she seemed to believe what she was being told. But she had not known that her husband sleepwalked until then – were they not deceiving her a second time? She remained convinced of it. From then onwards, she could not look at her husband without feeling a shudder of horror. She loved him deeply but was ashamed of it, as if it were a crime.

For a month she was so painfully torn between her conscience and her love that it visibly affected her health. When the Comte noticed the signs of the fever that was consuming her, he thought she might die from it and his suffering then reached its peak, as he feared he would be a murderer for a second time.

In his despair, he resolved to die himself and avert the death of this innocent and adored woman, but when he considered that his suicide, should it be declared as such, could have a tragic effect on Béatrix, he decided to go and ask Doctor Charrière for his assistance. After an anxious and sleepless night, he went to visit the old doctor.

He was welcomed into a modest practice, where everything exuded restraint and economy of the strictest kind. There was nothing on the tiled floor but a thin bulrush mat, upon which the doctor rested his feet. Books and surgical instruments were spread haphazardly across a table. There were armchairs covered in Utrecht velvet so worn that it was almost threadbare and a bookcase adorned with twill curtains and topped with plaster busts of famous scientific figures: this was the practice of one of the most celebrated doctors of the period. Doctor Charrière gave the earnings he received from his wealthy clientele to charity, while he lived as frugally as a miser. He was sitting at his table, busy with some scientific task.

'I have come, my dear Doctor, to ask you a great favour,' said Monsieur de Montbarrey, in a troubled voice.

'I am at your disposal.'

'I have come to ask you,' the Comte went on, with what seemed like great effort, 'for a poison that will end my life, without leaving any suggestion of suicide. My wife does not believe I am innocent, I can tell; my love frightens her and she is horrified by me, yet she loves me and blames herself for my crime. Affection and remorse thus divide her heart. She is suffering, and she tactfully hides her suffering from me, but I fear she will die from it. And so I want to prevent this awful tragedy with my own death.'

'She loves you, you say, and you think that your death would save her?'

'I hope so. When I am gone, she will gradually forget …'

'If you believe that your presence is causing her suffering, why do you not separate?'

'Live apart from her!' cried the Comte. 'Oh! You do not know how much I love her! And besides, is it not enough that I have united the life of this young, virtuous woman with my odious existence? Does loyalty not demand that I give her back her liberty, at least?'

'My lord,' replied the doctor coldly, 'there is no way that I can go along with what you ask of me.'

Monsieur de Montbarrey rose and paced about in agitation. Then he returned and sat back down opposite Doctor Charrière. 'Doctor,' he said, 'I say it again, Béatrix's life is at stake. But, even if I was the only one suffering, and my wife was eventually able to bear my presence and find consolation then I would still wish to die, so as to rid myself of the remorse that haunts me.'

'Your remorse, as I have told you, seems to me excessive: there can be no responsibility where there is no free will. But I admit that you are guilty up to a certain point. Do you thus think that a crime can only be redeemed with another crime, and that atonement is impossible? If, as you say, it was love that made you a guilty man, then make love your motive once more. Rather than pursuing a pointless death, regain the trust and esteem of the woman you love by doing good. Use your fortune and your time to help the poor; and, to rid your worried mind of the thoughts that torment it, work: devote yourself to the study of useful knowledge. Though today I refuse to assist you in committing a crime, I will, on the other hand, do everything in my power to help you in your attempt to make amends, and I will gladly put my considerable experience at your service. Finally,' he added, encouraged by the Comte's silence, 'have the strength to separate from your wife for a short while. This will restore her calm and give her time to forget the disastrous effect your revelation has had on her. Perhaps one day you will return to her with peace in your heart.'

In his words, full of great wisdom and generosity, Monsieur de Montbarrey glimpsed a solution to his troubles. He felt a profound sense of relief. He took the doctor's hands, and, grasping them effusively, thanked him for his advice and promised to put it into action immediately.

V

A few days after his visit to Doctor Charrière, Monsieur de Montbarrey secretly left his house and had a letter given to the Comtesse:

Farewell, Béatrix. I am leaving, because I understand the terrible torment you are suffering. I fill you with both horror and pity. You love me, and yet my love terrifies you. We must part. This conflict is breaking you and will destroy you in time.

Go back to a life of tranquillity and leave the sorrow to me. If I had been the only unhappy one, I would have been able to stand my hardship, because the sheer bliss of your love outweighs the suffering I endure. If I had to choose, I would still prefer an existence of endless anxieties and joys to a quiet life deprived of your tenderness. But seeing you suffer is more than I can bear. When this morning, having slipped into your room while you slept fitfully, I saw that your beautiful face was full of pain and your eyes were red with tears, I experienced a torment that I cannot describe.

It was in vain that you were silent about the unrest in your soul, for I noticed it in your quivers of fear when I came near, in your anxious expression, and in the sudden repulsion you displayed despite your best efforts, as if a bleak thought had just crossed your mind.

At one point, I wanted to kill myself so as to give you back your liberty, but Doctor Charrière, a wise, good man, whose mission here on earth is truly providential and who devotes his intellect and fortune to helping the poor, made me realise that this extreme course of action might put you in a dangerous position. He also helped me see that there might be a chance of repairing the ill that I have unintentionally brought about.

I had to change tack. I will have the courage to live and to undertake the gruelling task of atoning. I am in the prime of life and feel full of energy.

And so I have come up with a plan to use my life and my energy, hitherto ignored, to help my fellow creatures, based on the doctor's advice. I hope this occupation will bring me peace of mind, but, above all, I hope that my absence will restore calm to your heart, and that gradually, knowing that I am busy making amends, you will forgive me for the life I made you lead.

Farewell, then! I am taking with me your portrait and a lock of your hair. I cut the lock this morning while you were

*fast asleep, weakened by several sleepless nights, and I drank
in your beauty for the last time.*

*Farewell again. Determined as I am, my heart is breaking
as I write this letter, and tears blur my vision.*

But it is vital that we separate.

*Every time I do a good deed I will write to you, because it
will have been inspired by your memory.*

*Do not leave me without news from you, either. Your
letters, however infrequent they may be, will give me courage.
They will also give me the strength to resist the temptation
of seeing you again.*

Farewell, farewell! Forever farewell!
Gaëtan

VI

It had been a year and several months since the Comte and Comtesse de Montbarrey had parted ways. The Comtesse had closed up her house on Rue de Bellechasse and retired to the countryside, deep within the Franche-Comté mountains, hoping that solitude would relieve her sorrow. Yet, left to her dark thoughts and spending entire days immersed in distressing daydreams, she had sunk into a lethargy which had already dimmed her vital spark.

As for the Comte, he had cut off contact with the world and transformed his town house on Rue de Babylone into a large infirmary, where he took in and cared for the poor, infirm and sick. He roamed the working-class and destitute areas of Paris accompanied by Doctor Charrière, coming to the aid of every unfortunate soul he found there. He was unstinting in his efforts and devoted himself entirely to his task of making amends.

Love was what spurred the Comte on. The memory of Béatrix inspired everything he did. When someone he had helped expressed their gratitude, he would say, 'My friend, it is thanks to Madame de Montbarrey that I have done what I have done for you; and so offer your appreciation and blessings to her, from the bottom of your heart.'

Doctor Charrière, whose noble soul and charitable heart had led him to consider economic questions, had long known that occasional alms were inadequate, providing the poor with effective relief for a little while but leaving them vulnerable to future poverty. He had for many years sought to find a more lasting way of improving the lives of the working class. He thought he had found the answer, but his struggle to obtain capital had held him back. When he found that the immensely wealthy Comte de Montbarrey shared his concerns and ideas about organising aid, he presented him with his plan. The Comte agreed enthusiastically and provided his friend with the sum he thought necessary for his generous solution.

Architects, labourers and builders were put to work immediately, and soon, on a large plot in a neighbouring *département* that was perfectly suited to the task, they constructed a building which was a farm, factory, school and almshouse. From then on, this was where Monsieur de Montbarrey and Doctor Charrière sent the unfortunate people they saved from destitution or death every day, instead of throwing them out on the street without bread or shelter. There, elderly people could receive the care that their age or infirmity demanded, and children an education that developed their physical strength, helped determine their vocation, whether it was in industry or agriculture, and built up their morals.

A kilometre away from the main building, surrounded by tall trees, was a charming villa, built according to modern ideas of taste and elegance. This house was the realisation of the Comte's cherished dream.

Through his useful and charitable endeavours, the Comte had emerged from the limbo in which an incomplete education and a lifetime of frivolous pursuits had left him, for often the most beautiful minds need only a particular circumstance, a lever, a motive, to break free of that which holds them back. In Monsieur de Montbarrey's case, that motive was passion – and remorse.

The rejuvenating influence of his new way of life had gradually transformed the Comte, and he seemed to have taken on a new youthfulness. Health had erased the premature wrinkles from his face, and a look of serenity had replaced his sad expression. Activity seemed key to his robust manner, fortifying him rather than wearing him out. He had one of those strong constitutions that meant that the more he attempted, the less tired he felt.

On a beautiful, clear May morning, Monsieur de Montbarrey went into his study. The modestly furnished room looked on to a vast garden. The Comte opened the window and gazed outside. The countryside was alive with laughter and singing. Well, nothing inspires love and the desire for happiness like a beautiful spring day. His thoughts automatically returned to the Comtesse's departure. He was suddenly seized by a desire to see her again that was so intense that it took all his courage and resolution to resist.

He left the window and went to draw back a curtain, thereby unveiling the attractive portrait of a woman. It was the Comtesse. He gazed lovingly at it for some time, then took from his writing desk a packet of letters which he kissed with the passion of a man of twenty. He leaned on his table and began, for perhaps the hundredth time, to read the letters. When he had finished, he wiped his tear-filled eyes and rang the bell. A servant entered.

'Jean,' said the Comte, 'would you like to see Montbarrey, your village, again?'

'As your lordship wishes,' replied the servant.

'Well! You have eight days; leave at once. Go to the castle and try to get a glimpse of the Comtesse without her noticing. Look at her closely, so that upon your return you can tell me if she has changed, if she has grown thinner or paler, if she seems sad or happy. Go, then, and take not one day more.'

Jean left.

During that time, which seemed unbearably long to the Comte, he could think of nothing else. On the morning of the eighth day, the servant returned.

'So, Jean,' the Comte said, 'did you see the Comtesse?' And, when Jean hesitated to reply, he continued, 'Well, did you not manage to catch sight of her?'

'I'm sorry, my lord.'

'So, speak then. What did you see?'

'The Comtesse,' replied Jean, 'was unwell when I arrived at the castle. I followed your lordship's orders. Madame is too weak to walk, so I hid behind a flowerbed in the garden so I could see her when they pushed her chair through the gallery.'

'And?' asked Monsieur de Montbarrey, anxiously.

'Ah! My lord, I would not want to cause you sorrow.'

'Speak, then!'

'The Comtesse is much changed, and at first I could not believe that it was really Madame, who was once so beautiful and radiant.'

'Perhaps it was not her?' continued Monsieur de Montbarrey, trying to convince himself.

'I beg your pardon, my lord; I eventually recognised her,

because she still has such nice eyes, but how sad they were! I could not stop myself from crying at the sight.'

'I see, thank you! That's enough, Jean; please leave,' said the Comte, no longer able to contain his emotions.

Once the servant had left, he thought to himself, 'My wife is ill, perhaps dangerously ill. There is no time to lose.' He rang the bell and another servant appeared. 'When Doctor Charrière arrives,' he said, 'ask him to come to my study.'

Fifteen minutes later, the doctor entered. The Comte told him his fears and they decided to leave for the Château de Montbarrey straight away.

VII

The Château de Montbarrey was in one of the most picturesque parts of Franche-Comté and had recently been rebuilt in a modern, fashionable style, upon ancient feudal ruins. The main building was flanked by four identical turrets and was separated from the glasshouses on the left and the outbuildings on the right by two vast courtyards. In a marble basin in the front courtyard, four caryatids held a basket of flowers from which a jet of water spilled down in a misty spray. Majestic plane trees, bushy lime trees and acacias with feathery leaves bathed the entire courtyard in cool shade.

The main façade of the chateau extended out into the gardens and was made up of two galleries, one on top of the other. The upper gallery was supported by bronze pillars with cobaea, graceful morning glory and fragrant Spanish violets winding around them. There were jardinières lining the galleries, their bright, scented flowers visible behind a bronze balustrade as exquisitely crafted as lace. The chateau walls were completely covered with the supple stems of climbing rose, Virginia creeper, fragrant honeysuckle, purple trumpet vine and blue wisteria. In spring, there was something magical about the place. It looked like a palace of flowers.

A little below the chateau, in the middle of a lawn dotted with flowerbeds and clumps of trees, was an ornamental lake with an enormous fountain. The surrounding gardens were crossed by fickle streams, murmuring waterfalls, jagged caves of volcanic rock, dense thickets and secret pathways.

It was the end of May. Around two in the afternoon, a mail coach came to a stop a little way from Montbarrey. The Comte and Doctor Charrière got out. A servant let them into the grounds through a small hidden door for which he had the key. The Comte had so far said nothing and the doctor had respected his silence.

When they were close to the chateau, Monsieur de Montbarrey asked the servant: 'So, are you sure that the Comtesse is usually on the balcony at this time?'

'Yes, my lord.'

'Could you hide me somewhere I can see her, without her seeing me? Then take my friend to the chateau, where we will wait until the Comtesse is ready to receive us.'

They carried on walking in silence. As they drew nearer, the Comte's emotion was clear to see from his pale face and nervous step. The guide came to a stop as he led them down a pathway.

'It is here, my lord, that you must hide.'

Monsieur de Montbarrey followed the servant. By moving carefully from one flowerbed to the next, they soon reached the thicket closest to the chateau. Then, stopping again, the guide gently drew the branches apart and said to his master: 'From here, your lordship has a perfect view of the Comtesse.'

Then he left, and Monsieur de Montbarrey, putting both hands over his heart to stop it beating so loudly, went up to the opening the servant had indicated.

The Comtesse was sitting on a chaise longue, dressed in a sky-blue peignoir. Her hands were an unhealthy shade of white; her gaunt face expressed unspeakable melancholy. The light played across her translucent skin, which was dull with sickly bluish hues. Her sad eyes were fixed on the top of the fountain; she seemed to be studying its thousand sparkles and counting its glittering droplets. Despite her apathetic pose, she retained the touching gracefulness, the lovely elegance and the charm that animates the slightest movements of a woman in love.

Monsieur de Montbarrey had been watching her for a while, in a sort of intoxication full of tumultuous yearning, when she moved in her chair so that one of the balcony's balusters obstructed her husband's view. The Comte's eyes automatically followed the attractive face which so fascinated him, and forgetting all good judgement, he leaned forward out of the foliage he had been hiding behind.

The Comtesse met his eye and recognised her husband. She let out a cry, stood up in spite of her frailty, and fell back into her chair, lifeless.

A few moments afterwards, the unhappy Comte and Doctor Charrière were attending to the unconscious Béatrix. They carried her on to the bed in her room.

'Curses! I have killed her too! I have killed her!' he repeated hopelessly.

'You must leave,' said the doctor, 'as the Comtesse is extremely weak, and may experience another shock upon seeing you again. It might even be good,' he added, 'if she lost her memory for a while.'

When the Comtesse came round, she confided all her heartache to Monsieur Charrière.

'Doctor!' she said. 'He is here! I saw him again! And his presence, that I so yearned for before, is causing me dreadful pain! How I am suffering! I love him, but I cannot overcome the repulsion that he inspires in me, as even after everything you have told me, I am still not convinced that he is innocent. How can I believe that he has had only two episodes of sleepwalking since I have known him! You can see, Doctor, that I am consumed by these doubts, and they will soon be the death of me; because, I tell you again,' she added through bitter tears, 'I love him, but I am frightened of loving a criminal. I cannot look at him without shuddering with horror. He can see my struggles, he can sense them, he finds them even more painful perhaps than I do ... So, tell him that he must leave, that I do not want to see him again, and bid him my final farewell. I can sense that I have only a short time left to live.'

Monsieur Charrière did not attempt to change the Comtesse's mind. 'She needs proof that her husband really does sleepwalk,' he thought to himself, 'but what proof?' He appeared stricken. He thought about it for a long time, his head in his hands. Then, suddenly, he got up. His eyes were ablaze with hope. He went down to join the Comte.

'My dear friend,' he said to him, 'I have come to prepare you for a great tragedy.'

Monsieur de Montbarrey listened in silent dread. He had remained at the chateau but had been careful to stay out of his wife's sight.

'The Comtesse does not want to see you again,' the doctor went on. 'She cannot believe that you are innocent. You horrify her. She has therefore asked me to bid you farewell, because she can sense that she has only a few more days left to live …'

'Is her condition really that serious?' asked the Comte, in a choked voice.

'Alas!' replied the doctor. 'There is no hope any more.'

For a moment, Monsieur de Montbarrey was dumbfounded with sorrow. Then he let out an anguished sob.

'So I will be twice a murderer!' he cried.

'I'm afraid so,' said the doctor, with the dispassionate cruelty of a surgeon operating on a patient to save their life. 'After your doubts about the death of your first wife, it would have been wiser not to remarry.'

'If you are accusing me, my friend, I must be guilty!'

Monsieur Charrière did not reply.

The Comte was plunged into dreadful despair, but instead of consoling him, the doctor sought to upset him even more. Monsieur de Montbarrey was changing before his eyes: in the space of a few days his hair turned white, his eyes became sunken and his clouded gaze shone with a feverish glare. The doctor observed these changes, at first with satisfaction, and then with real worry.

Meanwhile, he was giving the Comtesse the most effective treatment to prolong what was left of her life. But this did not have the desired effect. He had run out of ideas, and he was overcome by a sense of powerlessness. Béatrix was going to die.

He told Monsieur de Montbarrey, who did not seem much troubled by it. 'The Comte has made his decision,' thought the doctor. 'He will kill himself straight after his wife dies.'

Nevertheless, when Monsieur Charrière was at the patient's bedside one evening, watching her sleep, he too gave in to the

148

fatigue that was creeping over him. Béatrix awoke in the middle of the night and her thoughts naturally returned to the memory of her husband. 'How miserable he must be!' she thought to herself. 'He has probably left, never to return. And yet, if he were innocent ...! But, no, it is impossible ... Oh Gaëtan, I will never see you again! I am so weak, so unwell! I will die without having told you that I believe in your innocence, if you are indeed innocent; or that, were you guilty, I absolve you in my heart!'

The doctor woke up while the Comtesse was experiencing these distressing thoughts. He did not notice her restlessness and was about to go back to sleep when suddenly, in the silence of the night, he heard a dull noise from the bedroom next door. Trembling, he listened. It sounded like a man's footsteps. The doctor felt extremely apprehensive.

The door finally opened. He thought he recognised the Comte and turned away in his armchair, closed his eyes, pretended to be asleep, and, quivering with emotion, waited to see what would happen.

When Béatrix heard the door opening, she turned over, and in the dull glow of the nightlight, could make out a man in the apartment coming towards her. She was terrified at first, but when she recognised her husband, her cry died upon her lips. She noticed that he was holding the lock of hair he had taken from her while she was sleeping on the morning of the day he had left.

'Is that you, Gaëtan?' she said, in a voice shaking with emotion.

The Comte continued to walk towards her and did not reply. When he was near the bed, he kneeled down. 'You called me, Béatrix,' he said. 'I was in bed, sleeping, and yet I heard your voice, because the lock of your hair that I placed upon my heart before going to sleep created a magnetic connection between us.

You wanted to absolve me. So then forgive me. Your forgiveness, like that of a deity, will ease my conscience; it will calm the remorse that is weighing me down.'

As he was speaking, Béatrix recognised the strange tone of voice and the glassy, staring eyes that had struck her once before. She remembered the fated night that Gaëtan revealed his unwitting crime to her. And how could she explain that her husband had known what she was thinking from far away and had answered the call of her heart? It confirmed the extraordinary things she had heard about sleepwalking. She finally understood. There was no doubt about it, the Comte really did sleepwalk. He had not been guilty, just unlucky. Happiness brought her strength back and she threw her arms around her husband's neck.

'Gaëtan,' she said aloud. 'Gaëtan, wake up.'

But the Comte was still asleep, and Béatrix felt a burning tear fall upon her hand.

'I forgive you,' she went on, 'and I shall believe in your innocence from now on.'

The doctor gazed in silent satisfaction upon the scene he had helped bring about by provoking the Comte. But when he saw that Madame de Montbarrey could not wake Gaëtan from his sleep, he became worried that it was taking too long. He took a glass of water, went up to the Comte and threw it in his face. The sleepwalker started, blinked several times and woke up.

VIII

Béatrix rapidly recovered, thanks to happiness, love, peace of mind, a desire to live and the care of the excellent doctor. Two weeks after the events recounted, she made a full recovery.

Monsieur and Madame de Montbarrey spent the rest of the season in the countryside, in the bliss of a second honeymoon. Then, in autumn, they went back to Paris. The Comte returned to his charitable work, admirably assisted by Béatrix.

In winter, they returned to society, but only very occasionally, because happy love shuns noisy festivities.

They finally took up residence in the Comte's villa the following spring, which he had kept as a surprise for his wife.

ASPHYXIA

VIOLETTE LEDUC

Translated by Derek Coltman

In a small French town, a young girl grows up under the hard blue gaze of a mother who will not hold her hand. Her only comfort lies in the warmth of an ill grandmother.

Yet the world around her is full of curiosity. From the obsessive Madame Barbaroux and her endless spring cleaning, to the homeless Monsieur Dezaille and his beloved collection of saucepans, Leduc reveals the eccentricities of provincial life with unflinching candour and striking beauty.

An extraordinary tale of a stifled childhood and an unrelenting love of life from the protégée of Simone de Beauvoir.

Asphyxia is a new edition of Derek Coltman's 1970 translation *In the Prison of Her Skin*.

VIOLETTE LEDUC was born in Arras, France, in 1907, the illegitimate daughter of a serving girl who would later blame Violette for her personal misfortunes. She was sent to boarding school, from which she was eventually expelled after her affairs with a female pupil and a tutor were discovered. Her 1964 memoir *La Bâtarde*, a frank depiction of lesbianism, poverty and loneliness, sold over 150,000 copies and nearly won the Prix Goncourt. Leduc died in 1972.

ISBN: 9781913547059
eISBN: 9781913547080

THE WOMAN OF THE WOLF
AND OTHER STORIES

RENÉE VIVIEN

Translated by Karla Jay & Yvonne M. Klein

A woman rides crocodiles like horses. A queen gives up her throne for her dignity. And Prince Charming is not who you might think . . .

The Woman of the Wolf and Other Stories, written in 1904, is perhaps the finest work by sapphic poet Renée Vivien. Blending myth, fairy story and biblical tale, Vivien creates powerful portraits of strong women who stand up for what they believe in – and of the aggrieved men who trail behind them.

Bold, defiant and suffused with a unique poetic voice, this scintillating collection of short stories offers a radical alternative to traditional lore.

RENÉE VIVIEN was a British poet who wrote in the French language. Born Pauline Mary Tarn in London in 1877, she spent most of her life in Paris, where her circle included the likes of Colette and Natalie Clifford Barney. She soon became established as one of the finest second-generation Symbolists. She died in 1909 at the age of thirty-two.

ISBN: 9781910477946
eISBN: 9781913547066

CPSIA information can be obtained
at www.ICGtesting.com
Printed in the USA
LVHW011054231120
672428LV00004B/5